The Extra

The Extra

KATHRYN LASKY

CANDLEWICK PRESS

Copyright © 2013 by Kathryn Lasky

First edition 2013

Library of Congress Catalog Card Number 2012955181
ISBN 978-0-7636-3972-3

13 14 15 16 17 18 BVG 10 9 8 7 6 5 4 3 2 1

Printed in Berryville, VA, U.S.A.

This book was typeset in Dante.

Candlewick Press
99 Dover Street
Somerville, Massachusetts 02144

visit us at www.candlewick.com

For the victims of Nazi persecution, including the Romani people of eastern Europe

VIENNA

Early Autumn 1940

One

Disappeared? What are you talking about? People don't disappear. She just went someplace."

"So where do you think Mila went? Why wasn't she in school? Today of all days, recitation day. She had been practicing forever. She was sure to get the prize."

"Maybe she's sick."

"Mila sick? Never—she's healthy as a horse. And even if she is, she would have dragged herself to school. No—something's fishy."

Lilo shut her eyes. If only Hannah didn't live in the same neighborhood. Then they wouldn't have to walk home together. She was always thinking the worst. It was too depressing. There was something slightly perverse about her. She seemed to almost enjoy bad news. There was always this "I told you so" attitude.

"I think the Nazis got her," Hannah said. "Your fingers still purple?"

Two weeks before, Lilo's family and all the other Gypsies over the age of fourteen in Vienna had been required to report to the police headquarters to be finger-printed. It was all part of the Nazi laws, the Nuremberg Laws. Now the Nazis knew who they were and where they lived. That was frightening.

"Uh . . ." Lilo hesitated. "I really haven't tried to wash it off."

"Lilo! Are you telling me you haven't bathed in two weeks, washed your hands in two weeks?"

"No, of course not!"

"Well, I can see they are still purple."

"So why did you ask?"

Hannah shrugged. "Well, I have tried to get it off. My mum, my dad, my brother, and I have tried everything—spirits of camphor, nail-polish remover mixed with scrubbing salts. Nothing works."

Lilo took a sharp left. "Hey, where you going?" Hannah said. "Home is straight ahead."

"My father's shop. I forgot he wanted me to stop by."

"All right, hope I see you tomorrow. I mean I hope we both see each other tomorrow. Could be you. Could be me." She shrugged again.

"Maybe Mila will be back," Lilo replied.

"You know she's not the first to disappear. An upper-grade girl, Zorinda, is gone, too."

But Lilo didn't want to hear any more of it. The church on the corner ahead marked the intersection of the street they were on and the one for her father's shop. Kirches-trasse was a cobbled lane more than a street. She rushed down it and turned in under the sign of the clock. On the window was a seal, the seal of the Imperial Clockmakers Guild of Vienna, with three stars designating him as a master clockmaker and licensed dealer in antique timepieces.

"Papa!" she called out as she came into the small shop that was not much bigger than a closet. A chorus of ticking clocks and all kinds of watches greeted her. The sounds of the timepieces stippled the air.

"Papa!" It was more of a yelp than a cry. The shop was open, but he wasn't there.

"Papa!" she now bellowed. She heard footsteps.

"What in the world!" Her father came through a back door.

"Where were you? I was so worried."

"I'm fine — I'm here. What were you worried about? Can't a fella take a leak? I just went to the toilet."

She smiled. Everything was all right. Her father stood before her, the little green eyeshade he always wore pushed up, the jeweler's loupe hanging on the black ribbon around his neck, his tie tucked into his vest so it would not interfere as he took apart and put back together all manner of watches and clocks. His fingers were still purple, too, she noticed.

"Papa, do you have any of that lubricating oil you use for the escapement wheels?"

"Sure, but what do you want with that?"

"I had an idea that maybe if we mixed it with alcohol, we could remove the stains on our fingers."

"Doubtful, but if you want to try, go ahead."

She stood over a small basin and poured the oil first and then the alcohol. "Can I use this sponge?"

"Sure. I'll be finished here in a couple of minutes. Then I just have to pack up a few things to take home to work on. The baron is coming by tomorrow for his watch."

"The tsar's watch."

"That's the one."

"Must be very valuable," Lilo said. She had now forgone the sponge and took up a wire brush that her father often used for cleaning his tools. She began scrubbing harder. "Ouch!"

"What's wrong?"

"Nothing."

A tiny bead of blood popped up where she had been

scrubbing. One of the wires must have stuck right through her skin. *Great,* she thought, *I'll probably get blood poisoning now from the damn purple dye going directly into my veins.*

Five minutes later, they were walking out of the narrow street and onto a broader avenue. "Feels like summer, doesn't it?" her father said.

"If only!" Lilo sighed.

"Don't worry. Summer will be here sooner than you think."

"It seems like a tease," Lilo said.

"What?"

"You know, when it's warm like this, but the days are growing shorter so fast. It's nine more months until summer, Papa."

"Ah, it will go quickly."

"Look at this!" her mother said as they came into the apartment. She waved a photograph in her hand. "From Uncle Andreas."

"Oh, let me see! Let me see!"

It was a picture of Lilo on Cosmos, the beautiful Lipizzaner. Suddenly summer seemed further away than ever. And Piber as far as the moon. Her uncle Andreas was the head trainer at Piber, the stud farm for the famous Spanish Riding School of Vienna. And every year they visited him for two weeks. With her uncle's coaching, she had learned to ride. It was on Cosmos's long back that she had mastered the first movement of the White Ballet, a classic in the Riding School repertoire. In Vienna only men rode the horses, but at Piber women were allowed to hack the old stallions that had been retired from stud services. She set the photograph on the table, propped up against a flower vase. Her mother came over and ran her hand across the back of Lilo's head. "Lovely picture, isn't it? Much better than the drawing I did of you on Cosmos."

"No, Mama, that's not so. You were trying to catch me when I was doing the first set of the dance steps. That was harder. Here Cosmos is standing still."

"Much schoolwork?"

"Some."

"Some?"

"Some, yes. That means between zero and much."

"Well, you should get started," her mother said, and gave her a pat on the head.

But it was hard to get started. The window was open, and a soft breeze blew through the lace curtains, sunlight casting an embroidery of shadows on the polished table. It was as if the low-angled setting sun of the autumn was determined to be remembered and make a show of itself. She traced the shadow design lightly with her pencil, careful not to mark the table. She set down the pencil and examined the stains on her fingertips. Dared she even hope about Piber?

Had her uncle Andreas been fingerprinted as well?

"Lilo!" her mother called. "Are you daydreaming?"

"It's too hot to study." Lilo looked at her parents. "There are kids out there swimming in the canal."

"Must be Roma girls," her mother muttered.

"Mama!" Lilo complained. "Look at Lori—she's Roma. You love Lori. She doesn't dress racy. She doesn't wear makeup. She is one of the smartest girls in the class, and her family does not travel around in a caravan. They live in an apartment twice the size of ours."

"She's an exception. And I bet you there's Sinti blood in that family somewhere."

Lilo sighed. Sometimes her mother was so narrow. "Look at Papa—he plays the violin at the best restaurant. Sinti aren't supposed to be musical, remember? Mr. Gelb is begging him to play more nights. Says he's better than Molder, who is Roma. So for all you know, we might have some Roma blood!"

"Lilo!" her mother exclaimed. "Fernand, did you hear what your daughter just said?"

"What?" he answered distractedly.

Lilo looked at her father. He was bent over the escapement wheel of the priceless antique watch of the tsar.

"She said maybe you have Roma blood, since you play the violin so well."

"Hmm, that's interesting." He was completely absorbed filing the teeth of the wheel. Lilo liked to hear the rasp of the file.

It was the rotation of the escapement that powered the timekeeping element. Her father wound it now and set it down to give it a try. A new sound. A tiny ticking as the wheel turned, allowing the gears to move, or "escape" a fixed amount with each tooth of the wheel. He'd fixed it! In some ways, to Lilo her father was a magician. He could fix time. Manipulate it. Save it!

Without the escapement, time would stop or perhaps run away, Lilo wasn't sure. When her father had explained this to Lilo when she was very young, she had imagined time running off like the gingerbread man. The tune and the lyrics began to run through her head now.

> *Run, run, run as fast as you can.*
> *You'll never catch me—I'm the gingerbread man.*
> *I ran from the baker and from his wife, too.*
> *You'll never catch me, not any of you.*

> *The baker made a boy one day,*
> *Who leaped from the oven, ready to play.*

He and his wife were ready to eat
The gingerbread man who had run down the street.

She always imagined pieces of watches—the gears, the jewels, the numbers on the face—running willy-nilly down the twisting streets of Vienna.

The ticking of two dozen or more timepieces chipped away at the quiet of their apartment. But there was also one other small sound that could be heard: the *puk . . . puk* as her mother pinned down bobbins of thread on a pillow for a new part of a lace design.

"What are you working on?" Lilo asked.

"Bridal veil."

Lilo got up from the table, leaving her math book open to the last problem. She walked over to the corner where her mother was working.

"Oh, it's beautiful, Mama."

Her mother looked up and smiled. "Thank you, Little Mouse."

Lilo made a face. "Mama, I am almost sixteen. How can you still call me Little Mouse?"

"It's a mother's prerogative. You can be fifty years old and I'll still call you Little Mouse. So there."

"So there," Lilo repeated with a sigh. "Who's it for? Someone rich?"

"Of course. Someone poor couldn't afford this. It's modeled after, or rather, inspired by, the veil that Princess Hélène of Orléans wore when she married the duke of Aosta in 1895," Lilo's mother explained.

Lace trading was a popular profession among Sinti women. And lacemaking was an ancient craft, practiced in Europe since Roman times. To know lace was to know history. And Lilo's mother knew lace. Some lace traders went door to door. Not Bluma Friwald. She dealt with fabric shops and high-end ladies' seamstresses and clothing boutiques, as well as fine table-linen stores and, of course, bridal fashion designers.

"Can I wear that when I get married?"

"Are you asking me to save some for you?" Bluma lifted her eyebrow as she looked at Lilo.

Lilo nodded.

"You know what you could buy with three meters of this, which is, by the way, a fraction of what Princess Hélène wore?"

"What?" *What will it be this time?* Lilo thought. *A month at the fanciest spa? A season ticket to the Opera House? A Leica camera?* It was a game she and her mother played.

"Maybe a Stradivarius," her father said with a chuckle as he bent over the watch with his jeweler's loupe. Her father had a good violin but not a Stradivarius, considered the finest kind of violin ever made.

"Your schoolwork almost done?" her mother asked.

"Yes, almost. Can't we go out for a walk along the canal or, better yet, to a movie at the Palace?"

"What's playing?" her mother asked. "If it's *Morocco*, please no, Lilo. We've seen it five times already."

"No, Mama, just four, and it's not *Morocco*. It's *The Holy Mountain*."

"Ach, your father's girlfriend, Leni Riefenstahl!" Bluma laughed. "She's Hitler's favorite filmmaker, Fernand. Are you sure she should be yours?" She winked at Lilo. "It's an old movie. Why are they bringing it back?" she asked.

"She should stick to those romantic mountain films," said Fernand. "And stop working for Hitler."

"No kidding," Bluma replied acidly. She focused very hard on tying a knot called the double rose, although it was not that complicated. Her jaw was clenched as if she feared she might say more.

"And how was school today, Lilo?" The studied casualness of Bluma Friwald's voice betrayed her anxiety. Lilo heard her father set down the tiny forceps he used to pick up the ruby jewel bearings for the balance wheels in the watch. A thick tension gripped the air.

"Fine." Lilo paused and thought of Mila but said nothing.

A year before, the Austrian government had started barring Gypsy students from public schools along with Jewish children. But so far, despite the fingerprinting, no Gypsy children had been barred from the school Lilo attended.

"You see?" Her father rose from his chair and, putting his hands on his hips, stretched back to ease the tension from sitting all day long. "What did I tell you? I'm still playing tonight at the café. They're not going after Sinti. Street musicians, yes. But a Sinti playing in the most expensive restaurant in Vienna? Not a chance."

"Be sure to thank Herr Gruniger for the lovely *Zwetschgenkuchen.*" Bluma nodded toward a tart with slices of rosy plums layered on top as perfectly as fish scales. The pastry chef from the Café Budapest often sent pastries home for the family.

Lilo wanted to believe her father's words. But Hannah's words came back to her. *Mila sick? Never—she's healthy as a horse.* And what about Zorinda? Two kids out did not mean that Gypsies were barred from her school. They were just out, absent. But there were always rumors. In a sense, the rumors did as much damage as the ordinances themselves. There were rumors that many Gypsies in Burgenland, Austria's easternmost province, had been deported to internment camps as part of something called the work-shy program. Work-shy? What a strange term it was. No one could ever describe her parents as work-shy. Herself possibly. Suddenly she no longer was inclined to go out for a walk.

"Are we going out, or aren't we?" her father asked, rolling his shoulders up to get the kinks out.

"Oh, I just remembered I have some more schoolwork to do."

She took a book from her bag. But it wasn't really schoolwork. So she supposed she was work-shy. It was a forbidden copy of a German translation of *Huckleberry Finn* with a different cover on it. Mark Twain and all his works had been banned, even burned at the great book burning in Berlin seven years before. But there was a black market for them. It was actually through Zorinda that she had gotten hold of the book. It wasn't hers to keep but hers to rent. For a pfennig a day she could have it. But if Zorinda was gone?

The author, Mark Twain, was the funniest writer in the whole world. In this chapter, Huck and Jim, the escaped slave, resumed their raft trip down the Mississippi. Lilo began by rereading her favorite parts, where Huck thinks about how wonderful it is to float down the river:

It's lovely to live on a raft. We had the sky, up there, all speckled with stars, and we used to lay on our backs and look up at them, and discuss about whether they was made, or only just happened.

She skipped to another page and read:

We said there warn't no home like a raft, after all. Other places do seem so cramped up and smothery, but a raft don't. You feel mighty free and easy and comfortable on a raft.

Free and easy and work-shy? The question hovered in Lilo's mind as she looked out the window to see the fading light over the canal and wondered if she would ever see the great Mississippi River. Her father said that the Danube might fit in the Mississippi's back pocket. She had laughed. It was something Mark Twain might say. A sudden harsh knocking on the door shattered her silent musings.

The rapping turned to a pounding. "Who knocks like that!" her mother said, half rising from her lace making.

Her father made his way to the door, his magnifying glass still in his hand. Opening the door, he gave a courteous little bow as uniformed men flooded in, their batons raised ready to strike. Fernand Friwald, though a fairly large man, seemed to shrink before Lilo's eyes. She looked around frantically. Her gaze fell fleetingly on the yards of lace fit for a princess, her father's violin, which was most certainly not a Stradivarius, the *Zwetschgenkuchen*.

Their boots are so shiny. The air was striped with the

dark polished gloss. There were only four men, but it seemed as if there were three times that many. Three of them weren't ordinary policemen at all but the dreaded SS, the *Schutzstaffel*, the paramilitary organization of the Nazi Party. One officer was barking something, but the words made no sense to Lilo: "In accordance with the decree issued on December 8, 1938, concerning the fight against the Gypsy plague . . ."

1938? It was 1940. And plague? What plague? Plagues were caused by rats and filth, Lilo thought. One could still smell the cedar scent from yesterday's floor waxing. The silver tea set gleamed. The windows sparkled. *We're Sinti. This is not supposed to happen. . . . My father is a member of the Imperial Clockmakers Guild. . . . You can't do this to him. To us. Papa . . .* Lilo wanted to scream the words that ricocheted through her head.

She wanted to say to these jackbooted SS men, "Look at this tart. It is from the finest restaurant in Vienna. They love us so much, they send home pastries every night Papa plays. Look at this lace—the lace of princesses, not dancing bears!"

The head jackboot, the one who seemed to be giving orders, was not from the SS. He wore the uniform of the local police. Lilo's eyes fastened on the tart. One of the SS men ambled over to the table and, sticking a fat finger into the center of the tart, scooped up a glob.

"Umm! *Zwetschgenkuchen*—ha, ha! *Zwetschgenkuchen* for the *Zigeuner.*"

She was yanked from where she stood, then shoved through the door. They were allowed to take nothing. But the fat-fingered man followed them down the stairs with a fistful of tart in one hand and a nightstick in the other. Lilo inhaled sharply when she saw the blood oozing from her father's brow. Why had she not heard the whack of that stick? Yet she was oddly aware of the most infinitesimally small details—a scuff mark on the stairwell hall she had not seen before, a jewel bearing caught in the cuff of her father's shirt. Everything came to her with a startling, surreal clarity. It was as if she were meant to register every detail, even the smallest ones, as from that moment on, her life would change irrevocably and forever. Fat Finger was still laughing about his joke. "Ha, ha! *Zwetschgenkuchen* for the *Zigeuner.*"

Two

"Together—*miteinander.*" That had become their prayer, their chant, their hymn. "As long as we are together, everything will be all right." Lilo's father said this at least thirty times a day. And they *were* together, with about five hundred other Gypsies, Sinta and Roma alike, in a barbed-wire enclosure at the Rossauer Lände police station and jail in Vienna.

"A quarter mile, no more, from the Café Budapest," her father also said even more often, perhaps fifty times a day. "If only I could get a message to Herr Gruniger."

"A pastry chef is no use in this situation," her mother had answered the first time her husband said this. But Lilo's father wouldn't give up. She noticed him now, studying a pigeon that had landed on the top of the barbed wire. She could almost read his mind. As a boy, her father had raised carrier pigeons. In their old apartment, the landlord had allowed her father to keep some on the roof. She had helped him tend to the pigeons, cleaning their cages. She had even learned how to attach the tiny canisters with the messages to their legs. Was he thinking of that now—of sending a message? she wondered. She felt a glimmer of excitement. Her father was resourceful, so full of ideas. He could fix things—watches, clocks—get them running again. She watched his face. He was thinking, thinking hard.

He sees that pigeon as a savior, a potential angel of deliverance. He must be wondering, Lilo thought, *if there is any way he could capture it, train it, and make it fly to the Café Budapest.* Could there be the slightest possibility? Her father turned away from the pigeon. *Don't! Don't turn away!* His face reddened with frustration, he kicked a small rock with his foot. That single gesture sent a shudder through her heart. Her father was such a patient, meticulous man. One had to be to do his kind of exacting work. It was as if at last he could no longer hold in the despair.

As it grew dark, floodlights came on.

"Oh, my God, look over there!" her mother said.

"Where?" Lilo asked.

"To the right, beyond the fence, up high."

Lilo gasped. How had they missed it? It was a huge billboard, and on it, floating eerily in the night, was the luminous face of Leni Riefenstahl. It was an ad for *The Holy Mountain*, the movie they had talked about seeing.

"Good God, there she is!" Lilo's father said, walking up to them.

The face was beautiful, almost unearthly, her mouth glossy and just partway open to reveal perfect teeth. Her eyes were dark and smoky and closely set, which gave her a somewhat beady look, almost feral. Yet there was a lovely delicacy to her face. Her high prominent cheekbones, the generous mouth, it all added up to a stunningly gorgeous movie star. There was something almost transcendent about that face, as if it belonged on Olympus with the gods. Her roles certainly reinforced this notion of a divinity. Her face loomed now in the night as bright as any moon. It was profoundly weird and discomfiting.

"I can't look at her!" Bluma Friwald said. Her voice was shaking. Fernand put his arm around her shoulders. They turned and walked to a shadowy corner of the enclosure. Lilo followed them. But there was no escaping. Other prisoners had begun to point at the huge billboard. "Ah! Leni . . . Leni Riefenstahl . . . I saw her in that movie . . . *Holy Mountain*, and then the other . . ."

Every day, more Gypsies were brought in, and every day, the conditions at the police station worsened. They all tried to stay as far away from the corner with the latrines as possible. The air was so foul, it was difficult to breathe. The rumors as to what might be in store for them multiplied.

The only thing they knew was that Rossauer Lände was a holding area for Gypsies facing deportation—a *Zigeunerlager*, a camp for Gypsies. For how long, they didn't know, and to where they might be deported was equally mysterious. There was talk of Lackenbach, an internment camp especially for Gypsies that was just nearing completion in eastern Austria. Another camp, Auschwitz, under construction in Poland, was also mentioned.

Lilo spotted Zorinda across the enclosure. She was talking with two other girls. As Lilo approached, Zorinda turned and gave her a big smile.

"Don't worry about the book," she said with a laugh. "But pretty good, isn't it? How far did you get?"

"Chapter eighteen. Huck's left the Grangerfords and is just meeting up with Jim again. They're getting back on the raft, back on the river."

Zorinda sighed. "We should be so lucky, eh?" She looked around. "Anyhow, let me introduce you. This is Michele, and this is Lola." She turned to the two girls and gestured at Lilo. "And this is Lilian, from my school."

"Just call me Lilo."

"So I was just saying that they're doing surgeries," Lola said to her.

"Surgeries?" Lilo asked. "What hospital are you talking about?"

"Ravensbruck," Michele answered. "Not a hospital."

Lilo thought that she might have heard of Ravensbruck. It was a camp. An all-women's camp. It would have been terrible if she and her mother had been sent there without her father. But in the next minute, she found out why there was an even worse reason. Michele exchanged a long look with Zorinda.

"She might as well hear it," Zorinda said.

"They . . . they do these operations on women so they can't ever have babies," Michele said.

"And not just grown women," Lola added. "They're doing it to small girls — girls as young as four or five."

Lilo felt all the blood suddenly drain from her face. It was as if the future had been erased, any *hope* for a future obliterated. Being in this barbed-wire cage was nothing compared with the utter darkness of the black wall of sterility, of a childless world, of a family that simply ended forever and ever. The Friwalds would be extinct.

"No! It can't possibly be true."

"It is true," Zorinda said, and clutched Lilo's hand.

"Why? Why would they do such a thing?"

"Because they don't want people like us to have babies. We aren't good enough to bring a new generation into the world. They think we are worse than criminals. That is why they didn't put us in cells. They didn't want us to contaminate the thieves, the murderers, the rapists who are inside those cells."

"How do we know if we are going to be sent to Ravensbruck or Lackenbach—or Buchenwald, for that matter?" Lilo asked.

"We don't," Lola said. "But we'll find out soon enough."

That night, shortly after midnight, glaring searchlights suddenly swept the enclosure. A series of harsh bleating noises came over the loudspeaker, and then the shrieking voice of the prison commandant: *"Achtung! Appell!"*

It was time for roll call. Lilo and her parents had been at Rossauer Lände for only five days, but they'd been introduced to roll call, *Appell,* on the first day. The prisoners were all to line up in rows of ten. Each prisoner was required to be in the same position each day, ready to be counted. Then some were called out for various tasks—cleaning latrines, digging new latrines, washing the tin plates and cups they had been issued, or ladling out the inedible stews. But never had there been a roll call at this hour of the night.

Lilo stood between her parents. They grasped hands.

Then they heard motors in the parking lot behind the enclosure. Dark-gray buses had pulled in. Emblazoned on the sides was the symbol of the Third Reich, now married to that of the Nazi Party: an eagle, its talons grasping an oak-leaf wreath encircling a swastika.

"Looks like we're taking a trip," someone whispered.

"Together—God let us be together," her father murmured, and grasped Lilo's hand so hard it brought tears to her eyes.

They filed out into the parking lot. The lot was not big enough for all of the buses. Lilo could see a dozen more lining the street. A long table was set up at the front of the lot. Police and SS officers sat behind it along with two men in civilian clothing and two women in nurses' uniforms. Lilo tried to figure out how it was decided which people were loaded onto which bus. The nurses would point to certain women and girls, who would be taken from the lines and escorted to a nearby bus. *That must be the Ravensbruck bus,* Lilo thought. *Anything but Ravensbruck! Please, God!*

Did her parents know about Ravensbruck? Lilo wasn't sure. She had not dared to tell them what the girls had told her. It was just too awful to imagine. She was afraid to look at her mother. Afraid that she might betray something that she knew and her mother did not. She wanted to protect her mother from the horrible thing that Zorinda and Lola and Michele had told her. There was a peculiar irony, Lilo realized. For although she might never be a mother, she felt this inexorable urge to mother her own mother, to protect Bluma.

They were drawing closer to the table. The starched nurses' caps seemed to take on a life of their own as the women bobbed their heads up and down, checking items off a list and then nodding for the next person to step up. Like strange white wingless birds, they nested in the darkness atop oddly disembodied heads, silently clucking. Should she shrink down between her parents or stand up tall. *No, stand up tall!* This was not a time to look invisible. They had to appear as a unit, inseparable, forged like the strongest metals, like iron.

It happened very quickly. One of the wingless birds dipped toward them. "*Nächste. Komm mal her, bis zum Schreibtisch*"—come up to the desk. Then another nod toward a bus as their names were checked off and the three of them were told to board bus number thirty. They were together! She felt her father ease his grip. Tears were streaming from all of their eyes. Just as they were boarding, she turned to look at the bus next to theirs, number twenty-nine. She gasped. Zorinda and Lola were both in a long line of women and girls. A nurse was hurrying them along. Zorinda caught sight of her. She shrugged, as if to say, "What a world we live in," then turned and stepped onto the bus. But all Lilo could think of was the Mark Twain book still sitting by her book bag. *Some Mississippi!* Then she grabbed her mother's hand and felt her father's hand drop onto her shoulder.

We're together! We're together. Miteinander! The word clanged in her head. That was all that mattered. *Miteinander.*

As the bus rounded the corner, they came directly under the billboard of Leni Riefenstahl.

"Would you look at that!" her mother said softly. Lilo did not want to look up, but she could not resist. It was as if the eyes were reeling her in, following her. The beautiful face rose in the night. The piercing dark eyes, the serene brow, the elegantly molded cheekbones. A luminous presence in the night—an angel? A goddess? But it was only Hitler's favorite movie star.

She heard the chimes of the clock tower in the nearby square.

"It's off," her father said, glancing at his watch, which he had somehow managed to keep. "Too fast."

Lilo suddenly thought of the gingerbread man. She pictured him running through the streets.

The baker made a boy one day,
Who leaped from the oven, ready to play.

He and his wife were ready to eat
The gingerbread man who had run down the street.

Except it was a gingerbread girl. Two gingerbread girls, Zorinda and Lola. "Run, run as fast as you can!" she whispered. The window fogged with her breath.

BUCHENWALD & MAXGLAN

Mid-Autumn 1940

Three

So what's this one?" The female overseer, the *Aufseherin*, scowled at the list on the clipboard. "Is she an *O* or a *G*? I'm not sure how to mark her."

Another woman bustled up and took the clipboard. "Just match her name to the number on her uniform," she barked.

"Ach! Here she is. That's an *O*. I know someone makes the *G*'s sometimes look like *O*'s. Sloppy. I'll talk to the intake secretary."

"All right, extend your left arm and don't wiggle. It's ink. I want it perfect." *Ink for what? Perfect for what?* Lilo wondered as the woman inscribed an *O* on her forearm. She had just been marked, marked like an item on the discount counter at the department store in Vienna. She had become an article, a commodity — branded! But for what?

"Now that is a nicely formed *O*," she said, still holding Lilo's arm. "I learned how to make my letters in school. Always got an A+ in penmanship." *And look where it got you!* Lilo thought. "What do you think?" the woman looked up brightly at Lilo as if expecting a compliment.

"I've seen better but not on human flesh," she muttered.

There was a gasp behind her. The *Aufseherin*'s face turned to stone. Then a slow smile crawled across it, making her lips look like fat worms. "All right, then"—the words oozed out slowly—"let me try again. Maybe I'll put more letters on you just to practice my penmanship."

"Aufseherin Liebgott," the matron who was standing behind her said, "there are still thirty more prisoners to be done."

The *Aufseherin* shrugged and waved Lilo on.

Lilo stared down at the *O*. Her rage surged.

As she rose from the chair and another girl was led in, Lilo looked at the matron who had gasped, but the woman avoided her eyes. She was pretty, very pretty. Slender and blond, neither young nor old, but there seemed to be a weariness about her that defied the obvious markers of age. No wrinkles, no gray hair. She shook her head slightly when Lilo passed by.

"Be careful," she whispered. *"Es gibt keinen Gott hier."*

But Lilo did not need to be told that there was no God in Buchenwald.

On her way back to the barracks, Lilo saw guards and some other prisoners moving cots into a building. A man in shiny boots with a ferocious dog at his side was shouting orders through a bullhorn.

"Come on, move! We've got to get forty beds in there. Stack them up. It's not a luxury hotel. We'll dig latrines tomorrow."

A woman next to her whispered, "We're the first women prisoners here, they say."

"Where are the men kept?" Lilo asked.

"Not sure," the woman replied. "But here. They are here." *Then Papa is here someplace,* Lilo thought.

"Did you see your father?" Bluma asked as soon as Lilo came back to the barracks. "No, Mama. They closed the curtain between the men's part and the women's."

"It was open when they did me." Bluma sighed, her shoulders slumped down.

"Well, he's here, Mama. Someplace in this camp. Maybe we can find him somehow."

"Let me see the mark on your arm."

"Why? It's ugly."

"I want to compare the letters. Maybe there's a letter on his arm — a code. Perhaps they give families matching letters so they know who belongs together."

"Mama, there are far more people in this camp than there are letters in the alphabet. All I know is that the numbers on our shirts match up with our names on the matron's clipboard. But the letters on our arms make no sense to me."

But Bluma was just staring at the O. She sighed. "There seems to be no rhyme nor reason."

Lilo blinked. It seemed the most absurd remark ever. "Rhyme nor reason! Mama, are you crazy? They are herding us around like cattle. Branding us with letters. You think there is a logic buried in this somewhere? You think it's our fault and if we had done something different, we could have saved ourselves?"

Bluma's eyes began to well with tears. Her mouth trembled as she looked at her daughter in dismay. Suddenly Lilo wanted to take back every word she had uttered, even if what she had said was true. She had never in her life spoken to her mother that way.

"Oh, Mama, I am sorry." She grabbed her mother and hugged her. Clung to her.

Her mother buried her head on Lilo's shoulder, and said in a low, guttural voice, "All that matters, Lilo, is that we keep track of him. We have to find out his letter or maybe the number on his uniform somehow. We are just letters now, Lilo. Letters that seem to have nothing to do with our names. No names here," she said softly, then added, "The ink erases us, but we can't erase the ink. How . . . how peculiar."

"I know, Mama. I know."

"Think of something. Think of anything. We must send him a message somehow. Tell him we are all right for now. And find out"—Bluma's voice faltered—"if he is, too."

Lilo began to bite her thumbnail. The pretty matron who had warned her to be careful—what was it she had said? *Es gibt keinen Gott hier.* Could she go to her? Could she be trusted? But what choice did she have?

But the good matron seemed to have disappeared for the rest of the day. It wasn't until that evening that Lilo caught sight of her as she walked by the barracks in Block 5 on her way to what passed for their evening meal, the same stew as at Rossauer Lände except perhaps slightly more edible, since it had been watered down to nothing. She waited in the shadows at the corner of the barracks and then stepped out.

"Oh!" Good Matron gasped.

"I'm sorry. I didn't mean to frighten you." A queer little smile fled across the woman's face. *Frighten. I frighten her?* Lilo thought. *How utterly stupid. No wonder she's smiling.* "I—I—" Lilo began to stammer. "I need to ask you something. A kind of favor." She saw the woman's shoulders sag when she said *favor*.

"Yes. Go on," the matron said softly.

"My father. We need to know if he's all right. I know there was a transport out of here last night. Was he on it? Is there any way you can find out? His name is Fernand Friwald. He's a watchmaker and he repairs watches, too — old valuable antique watches. He could be useful. He could work in a munitions factory. There is one near here. He does delicate, fine work."

The words began to pour from her mouth. The woman reached forward and placed her hand softly on Lilo's arm. She shook her head. It was at that moment that Lilo noticed the blood on the woman's uniform. A single large stain and then a few smaller ones. Lilo could not drag her eyes from the bloodstains. "Did you hurt yourself?" The woman looked confused. Then she saw what Lilo was looking at.

"Oh, that — no." But her bottom lip began to tremble. "Look, a name doesn't really help. I never go into the men's section, anyhow. The best thing you can do is stand near the fence on the east side of Block 16. That's where the men are permitted some exercise. You might catch a glimpse of him there."

For two days, every chance they got, Lilo and her mother would go to the fence to scan the throngs of men milling about in a containment yard. On the third day, a boy called out. He was on the other side of the fence when Lilo had gone on her work break from assembling the tracks of barbed wire.

"So whatcha looking for?" He spoke German but with a Roma accent.

"What's it to you?" Lilo was immediately suspicious. No one had ever spoken to her, let alone made eye contact with her, when she stood at the fence. Almost immediately after arriving at Buchenwald, she had noticed that none of the prisoners made eye contact. It was as if they were each in their own private hell. No trespassing allowed.

"No big deal. Hey, only trying to help." He spoke the fast, slangy jargon of the street. He raised his hands in mock defense. But he kept his eyes on her. She noticed that his eyes actually weren't really black but the darkest blue. She had never seen eyes that color.

"I'm looking for my father. I just thought I might catch a glimpse of him."

"So maybe I can help you."

"How?"

"Look, I've been around."

"Around? Around this yard?"

"My third camp in four years. I know how these places work." He puffed out his narrow chest as if he were wearing badges, like a decorated general in an army, an army of concentration-camp prisoners. "You want extra food, I can organize it. You want—"

"I want my father," Lilo said, cutting him off.

"So what's his name?"

"Fernand Friwald. He's bald and maybe just under six feet tall. He has a bruise on his forehead from where the SS hit him when they picked him up. My mother and I are so worried that he was shipped out in that last transport."

"Okay, okay. I'll check into it. What's your name?"

"Lilian—Lilo. Call me Lilo. And yours?"

"Django. Meet me here later on your next work break. I might even be able to organize some bread for you."

"Bread?"

"Yes. Look, just be here, all right?"

"I will." He began to walk away. "Hey, Django," she called. There was a note of desperation in her voice. He turned around. "He's a watchmaker, and . . . and we were hoping that they might let him work in the munitions factory."

"That would be very smart of them to do that, but who says Nazis are smart? But I'll find out." Lilo cocked her head to one side and studied him. Where did he get this uncanny confidence? And if he didn't know something, would he ever admit it? She doubted that he would. He was shorter than she was, thin as a rail, and looked as if he might blow away like a dry leaf in the slightest wind.

"What's wrong?" he asked.

"How do you do what you do?"

"What do you mean?"

"Get bread, get information — all that."

"Hey, did you see the sign on the iron gates?"

Lilo nodded and whispered the words, *"Jedem das Seine."*

"Yeah. 'To each his own,' or 'One gets what one deserves.'"

Lilo now realized that was what had irritated her when her mother tried to make sense out of the situation. It was as if she had been thinking they deserved this somehow.

"So what about your father? Did you find out anything?" Bluma asked when Lilo returned to the table in the barbed-wire assembly room, where they both twisted the barbs onto the lengths of wire. Lilo stared at her mother's hands.

"You cut your finger, your thumb."

"These pliers are lousy. I think they give them to us especially so we'll cut ourselves." Lilo kept staring at her mother's hands. Was it possible that two weeks before, those same hands had been making lace? It was as if their entire previous life had been some sort of chimera, a complete fantasy.

"Did you find out anything?"

"Not really."

Her mother looked up. "What do you mean 'not really'?"

"Shush, here comes the matron. We can't be caught talking."

Once the matron was well past, Lilo continued. "I met a kid. He seems pretty smart. He says he's going to look for him." She heard her mother catch her breath. Then she reached over with her hand and stroked Lilo's head.

"Thank God."

"Nothing's certain, Mama. Maybe he'll find nothing. But I told him what Papa looked like."

"And that he's a watchmaker? Did you tell him that he could be useful in the munitions factory in the next town? A lot of them work there, I think. And I hear they get fed well, too."

"Yes, Mama, I told him, and he says he'll bring me some bread."

"You're kidding."

"No. He said he could 'organize' it."

"Who is this boy?"

"Django."

"You mean like the musician Django Reinhardt?"

"Not old enough, but maybe he's related or something. He's Roma."

"Roma, Schmoma—who cares, if he can find out about your father?"

Lilo looked at her mother and smiled. "Yes, Mama. Roma, Schmoma, what does it matter?"

Four

Django shoved the piece of bread through the wire fence. But he did not meet her eyes. Lilo felt a dread swim up in her. Was this bread supposed to soften what was to come next?

He began to speak, still without looking at her. "I found him."

"You did! How is he?"

"He's . . . he's okay." He lifted his eyes slowly. "He's leaving tonight on a transport."

"Where? What for?"

"I don't know. I couldn't find out much. I think it's going east."

"East?" East was bad. East was where there were rumors of new camps. Camps that were not simply camps of concentration but extermination. It was said that they would need laborers to complete the camps.

"But that's not right. He can't be going there. What do they need with a fine watchmaker? They need my father at Krupps, Siemens. I'm telling you, he can do the finest work. He understands gears, escapement wheels. He could make those electrical switches. Siemens makes millions of those." Lilo babbled on as she threaded her fingers through the barbed wire.

"I know, I know," Django said softly. He wove this own fingers through and touched her knuckles.

"To each his own—the sign on the gate says it. This is Papa's own. He can do it."

Django just shook his head wearily. "Tonight at midnight, go around to the back of the barracks. You know where the rabbit hutches are?"

"Yes."

"They are using that drive to load up the transports. Be there at midnight. You might see him."

"All right." She opened her mouth to say something more.

"Don't thank me," he said.

A few minutes before midnight, Lilo and her mother made their way from their barracks as if they were going to the latrines. Behind the latrines, they cut toward the rabbit hutches. There were twenty or more of the small struc-tures that perched on short stilts so the rabbit droppings could fall out to the ground and easily be swept up. She heard small grinding noises.

"What's that?" she whispered to her mother.

Her mother tapped her teeth. "They grind them."

But there were also other sounds—soft cooings and then the occasional thumps. *What do they talk about?* Lilo wondered. Would it be preferable to be a rabbit, numb to any danger, any threat? Yes, they wound up in Nazi stews, but they never knew anything different until the moment their throats were slashed. They had probably been raised in captivity, had no memory of scampering through a meadow, all blowy with the scents of spring. If there was no memory, there could be no fear.

"Look!" her mother said.

Lilo's thoughts about rabbits were quickly replaced by the scene at the fence. Half a dozen women were huddled against the barbed wire—not just huddled, but embracing it. Lilo and Bluma joined them. They saw two parked transport buses. Then there were the sharp cries of the *Lageralteste,* the senior prisoner, and his chief *Kapo.* "Line up—ranks of five." It was the same formation as for roll call. Then the *Kapo,* one of the inmates who aided the Nazi commanders in exchange for certain privileges, began calling out numbers. And the men answered. There were perhaps sixty men in all, and when they were one-third of the way through the rolls, in the midst of the scores of prisoners answering *"Hier,"* they both heard one that made their hearts leap. "Look right there!" cried Lilo. It was Fernand Friwald. Like a shadow, he stood at the near edge of one of the lines. But the shadow had turned toward where they stood and shouted, *"Hier!"* The shadow had spoken, exclaiming that he was here to his wife and daughter.

"It's him!" Bluma whispered hoarsely.

Then the ranks of men began boarding the two buses and the shadow that was Fernand Friwald was swallowed into the dark hulk. The engines started. The gleaming swastikas emblazoned on the sides flashed in the moonlight.

Many of the women began to cry, but not Bluma Friwald. Her face was carved into a grim expression. As she clutched Lilo's hand, they made their way back to the barracks through the mewling, thumping, softly gnashing rabbits in their hutches.

Lilo looked up. It was a starry night. She saw a recognizable autumn constellation. Orion. It had been in Piber, far from the city lights, where she had first seen this constellation. Her father had taught her how to recognize so many. The swan and the dolphin and the little horse, which seemed like a guardian constellation special for

Piber. And now on this night there was Orion, the blind huntsman, who stumbled across the night sky. But the stars smeared in the night as she began to weep. There was certainly no God in Buchenwald, and if there was one in heaven, she thought he was as blind as the huntsman.

The next morning, their work detail was changed. Both Lilo and her mother were to report to the garden to dig for the winter root vegetables. This was supposedly a good detail. One could sneak carrots and potatoes and eat them raw. They had not been digging long when someone dropped onto the ground on her knees between them.

Lilo turned, expecting another inmate, but it was Good Matron.

"Listen to me. Don't say a word." She turned to Bluma. "A selection for the procedure is scheduled."

"Procedure?" Bluma asked. Lilo touched the O on her arm. Her mother had the same letter. There had been some discussion in the women's barracks about the meaning of the various letters that had been inked on their forearms. It was a code of some sort. It had been rumored that the letters might indicate a medical procedure. But no one could quite figure it out. Now Lilo knew immediately what Good Matron was talking about.

"What are you talking about?" Bluma asked.

The Good Matron now took Bluma's arm and tapped

the *O*. Lilo was astounded by her own blindness, her sheer stupidity. How had they never figured this out? How had they believed that such medical experimentation was said only to be done at Ravensbruck?

"Sterilization."

"I'm too old anyhow to have babies," Bluma said.

"They don't think that way, and your daughter isn't."

"They wouldn't!" Bluma's face froze into a mask of horror as she stared at the *O* on Lilo's forearm.

"They will. Today at noon, there is a selection. You might escape, but your daughter won't."

"B-b-but only at Ravensbruck. Not here," Lilo protested.

"They do all sorts of medical experimentation here. Why do you think they finally brought women in?" Good Matron replied.

"It can't be!"

"It will be. Believe me. I can't help you both, but I can help you." She looked at Lilo. "This detail ends in another hour. Meet me at the pig barn. It's right over there."

An hour later, Lilo was buried beneath a mountain of pig feces, and now she realized that although there was no God, there was this woman whom she had named Good Matron. Lilo knew she could no longer look to heaven but it would be on earth in a heap of pig shit that she found a divine spark of what used to be called humanity.

From the smelly camouflage, she could hear the voice of the camp commandant, Karl-Otto Koch, in the square as he proceeded with the selection. She could picture him walking with his two leashed dogs and most likely his red-haired wife, Ilse, at his side. There were terrible rumors about this woman and the things she did to prisoners — rumors about skin taken from dead prisoners to make lamp shades. Lilo swore she could hear the click of the woman's high heels walking across the pavement. The loudspeaker squeaked and hissed, temporarily drowning out the growls and barks of the dogs as the commandant began to speak.

"Listen to me, inmates. Today we shall be selecting two dozen of you to become medical pioneers. This will be your service to humanity, and those who volunteer quickly will be eligible for early release."

Don't believe them, Good Matron had warned. Those who resisted would be forced. Furthermore, Good Matron had warned that the dogs Commandant Koch walked with were specially trained to attack recalcitrant inmates.

Lilo was to stay buried until Good Matron came by whistling the melody of "The Watch on the Rhine," a favorite patriotic tune of the Nazis. But it had to be that song and not what had become known as the "Buchenwaldlied," the official camp song that was blasted through the loudspeakers every morning and evening. She could hear the commandant's voice extolling the marvelous wonders of the Reich's scientific endeavors. "You are to be a part of history!" He went on for what seemed like forever.

And then Lilo heard the voice of the commandant's wife, Ilse Koch. High and shrill, it seared the air. "Ladies — if I might call you Gypsy scum *ladies* — you still, we assume, have breasts. You still have genitals. . . ." Lilo pressed her fingers in her ears. She would stuff pig shit in her ears to block this woman's voice. *But how will I hear the song? I must hear the song.* So she took away her hands and waited. The shrill voice called out names: "Brenna Wilfmore, Alana Kranz, Elsa Reinhardt, Bluma Friwald." Every muscle in her seized. It was as if an electrical current had sizzled through her body. On and on it went. And then very clearly she heard the sound at last of Good Matron whistling the tune, and she came out from the pile of pig shit.

"What's this?" Lilo asked as she peered into what looked like a bucket of bloody guts that Good Matron had brought.

"Pig guts. Slather it between your legs."

"What?"

"Don't ask questions. Just do it. And here's a wet towel to wipe off the pig shit." Lilo started to speak. "Don't ask questions!" Good Matron hissed.

"It wasn't a question," Lilo said softly. "I . . . I just . . . I know you risked a lot. I don't want anything to happen to you—that's all."

"Just—just go ahead and do what I said." Good Matron's voice was breaking. She turned away.

When Lilo had finished, Good Matron sighed. "It might work. Just pretend you are bleeding for the next couple of days. Use your mother's cloths in your panties. She'll have enough blood for the two of you."

When Lilo returned to the barracks, the sight of her mother was so shocking that she felt her own legs start to give way. "Oh, Mama!" She could barely look. Her mother was crumpled up on the lice-ridden cot, too weak to speak. What seemed to Lilo like a puddle of blood pooled beneath her mother. Some of the blood had penetrated the cot and dripped onto the floor.

Two weeks later, Bluma was still bleeding when Good Matron came to them with news. "You're being trans-ferred. Stand up and look healthy."

"Why? So they can have more fun killing us?" Bluma asked.

"You're not going that far east. Not an extermination camp. Maxglan."

"Where's that?" Lilo asked.

"Austria, near Salzburg."

Again the buses came at midnight, but this time it was both men and women being loaded. Lilo caught sight of the boy Django. He gave her a thumbs-up as he spotted her across the yard, then half a minute later fell into a line with Lilo and her mother.

"Never miss a chance to travel with the ladies," he said, winking.

"What a card!" Bluma muttered.

"Mama, don't be that way. This is the boy who told me about Papa."

And now for the first time since Fernand had left, Bluma's eyes filled with tears. She turned to Django and embraced him.

"Thank you! Thank you." Her words were like gasps, and she seemed to be clinging to Django for dear life. Lilo watched her mother embrace him and felt an overwhelming sense of embarrassment. Of course her mother was grateful to him, but this seemed a bit excessive. There was the sharp blast of a whistle, the sign that they were to begin boarding the buses.

On the bus, Lilo and Django squashed into one seat so that her mother could have more room to almost lie down in the other seat.

He was a talker, this Django, and a joker as well. But he had an old man's face, Lilo thought.

"So, Sinti girl, you're not going to make a smelly

bear joke, are you? You know, Romas and their dancing bears."

"Why would I do that? Are you going to make music jokes?"

"I don't know. Isn't that what we are supposed to do? Sinti think they're smarter than Roma, Roma think they're better than Sinti."

"Very childish, I think," Lilo replied primly.

"No teasing, then?"

"Why would you want to tease?" Lilo asked, genuinely puzzled. But she began to notice that humor and grim sarcasm were Django's strategies for surviving. Buchenwald was just another stop for him over the past four years. He knew the game. He had learned the ways. One did not simply get food. One organized it, for indeed it was a major endeavor—figuring out the right guard to approach, one willing to break the rules. One had to be a genius at reading human nature, be able to detect the subtlest glimmer in a guard's eye that might suggest a trace of empathy, a hint of a moral conscience. And for this trip, Django had organized a hunk of cheese that he shared with Lilo and her mother.

"Maxglan," he sighed. "Now, let me think, what do I know about Maxglan? This will be my fourth camp."

"What was your first camp, Django?" Bluma asked.

"Ah, Marzahn, just outside Berlin—during the

Olympics, would you believe it?" He said this with such delight, as if he had had a front-row seat to every event. "You know, Hitler had to clean up the city, put a good face on things for all the visiting dignitaries and foreigners who came to see the games. So they rounded us all up to keep us out of sight."

"Your family?" Bluma asked.

His face turned dark. He stared straight ahead. He was no longer a spectator in the front row of the games. "Yes. My baby sister died in Marzahn. Then my father and brother and I were sent to Lackenbach—the rats were plumper there. My mother was sent to Dachau and . . ." He shrugged, and his voice trailed off. "But Maxglan, let me think a moment." He was quickly his old self again. "Lots of Roma there. I've heard through the prison grape-vine. So I might feel at home. Don't worry: I'll introduce you." He paused as if to think. Then, scratching his head, he mused, "Local industry. Well, of course there are the Salzburg marionettes. And Mozart—oh, they love Mozart around there. Whole square dedicated to him." Django talked on for some time. Lilo was just drifting off to sleep when she heard him say finally, "But I can't imagine why they would be dragging us all the way to Maxglan."

Five

The trip was hard on Bluma. Her dress was soaked with blood by the time they arrived the next day, and they only rested a few hours before there was another roll call.

"Get her up. She must be standing! Otherwise . . ." Django was hissing orders like a commandant. But Lilo knew he was right. If you didn't stand, if you didn't move, you were as good as dead. This stop, Maxglan, was a reprieve of sorts. They had gone east, but they had not crossed the border into Poland, where the most notorious of the extermination camps were rumored to be. Maxglan was, according to Django, halfway between a work camp and a holding area like Rossauer Lände. But it was not in Poland, and that was the crucial fact.

Lilo was beginning to realize that the phrase "Otherwise you'll end up in Poland!" was a story within itself. It did not need a preface, and the epilogue was death.

Lilo and her mother had briefly held out hope that Fernand Friwald might be at Maxglan, but they soon learned they were the first transport into Maxglan in the last two months.

It was chilly, and the evening swirled with rags of mist. Lilo glanced up at the watchtowers, where guards stood with rifles pointing down at them. She hitched her mother up by the elbow, then surreptitiously snaked her arm around her back so that it looked as if she had been crowded just a bit by her mother and the woman on the other side of her. "You can lean back on me, Mama. Not too much, or they might see I'm helping you."

She felt the slight weight sink against her arm. She could feel every bone in her mother's back.

"I don't believe it!" There was a hushed awe in Django's voice.

Then her mother's voice, just a soft exhalation of wonder. "His girlfriend!" She spoke as if in a trance.

Lilo turned her head in the direction they were looking and caught sight of a tall lady, dressed in fine wool slacks, carrying a briefcase.

"No!" Lilo whispered. "Her!"

As the beautiful face emerged from the night gauzy with fog, it was as if she had climbed out of the billboard.

Leni Riefenstahl was here at this stinking, run-down camp. There were two different realities colliding in the camp of Maxglan. It was not supposed to be this way, Lilo thought. Leni Riefenstahl belonged on the billboard, hovering in the moonlight of the clock-tower square, or on the movie screen in the Palace Theater, but not here — not here with them, dirty Gypsies, women still bleeding from terrible operations.

Two assistants preceded her and occasionally motioned for her to come take a closer look. Lilo guessed that there were more than 250 prisoners lined up. But she wondered what these three people were doing — the lady in the slacks with her briefcase and the two men not in uniform. She leaned around the woman who stood next to her and called to Django, who was standing next to another Roma boy, just a child really.

"Django, what is it?"

"Casting call." His dark eyes sparkled. She saw him bend down and whisper something to the small boy. The boy stood up straighter and squared his shoulders.

"What?" She had never heard these words. "What are you talking about?"

"The movies."

"Like Hollywood?" She saw the beautiful lady raise her hand to her face and close her thumb and forefinger to make an **O**. "What's she doing with her fingers?"

"Framing us—like in a camera lens," Django replied. "So look sharp, Lilo. Here she comes."

Lilo felt her mother slip down toward the mud. "I can't do it. I'm losing too much blood."

"You can, Mama! You can." Lilo gave her mother a sharp poke. She felt her mother gasp and straighten up. It was just in time. The woman was a few yards away, picking her way through the mud in her beautiful alligator boots. She carried a small notebook and sometimes paused to write something down.

"What do you think she is writing in the notebook, Django?"

"Oh, that you are pretty and perfect for a part."

"Don't be silly."

"Okay, that I am so handsome that I should play the lead."

"Yeah, you're a regular Clark Gable!" Lilo said.

The woman was walking more quickly down the line of prisoners. The face in the poster, the face of Leni Riefenstahl, was inches from her own.

"This one, Hugo. This girl." Then she again held her hand to her eye and closed her thumb and forefinger, and swung the "lens" directly at Lilo. She looked back at the woman through the **O** formed by her fingers. The eye glimmered darkly. Lilo would never forget that eye. Lilo found that she seemed in some uncanny way to know exactly what to do. She tilted her head saucily and pressed her mother closer, her head resting lightly against her mother's. Then she smiled so that her dimple flashed.

"Ah! *Liebling.*" Riefenstahl turned to the man called Hugo. "This one is charming."

"And my mother, too," Lilo said softly.

"Yes, clean them up. *Mein Gott.* I see lice crawling out from her hair." She continued down the line. "And this one and this." She pointed at Django and the little boy next to him. Lilo felt a sweep of relief that Django had been chosen. She saw him run his hands through the stubble of hair on the child's head. The gesture was so unimaginably tender that she nearly gasped aloud.

The next day, twenty-three of the Maxglan prisoners, including a three-month-old infant and its mother, were loaded onto two trucks. As the trucks rolled out of the camp, Bluma Friwald grasped Lilo's hand and shut her eyes tight.

"Mama, what are you doing?"

"I won't believe it until we turn."

"What do you mean?"

"You know what I mean. Turn right, we head east. Turn left, west."

A few seconds later, she felt her mother slide against her. "Mama, it's . . ." But her voice was drowned out as a roar went up from the two trucks.

"Next stop Hollywood!" Django yelled.

"Hollywood!" cried the little boy who was sitting next to him, and he punched the air with his stick-thin arm. They had turned left.

Not Hollywood, but the village of Krün, nestled at the foot of the Karwendel range of the Bavarian Alps. *West, but not as far west as California,* Lilo thought.

They were heading to the village that had been built for the set of the movie. The prisoners were told that Leni Riefenstahl, Hitler's favorite director, was making a movie called *Tiefland.* It was to be Leni Riefenstahl's first time directing a dramatic film rather than a documentary. The story was a romantic one, about a beautiful Spanish girl, based on a Spanish folk opera.

Since it was impossible to film in Spain or cast Spanish actors in the middle of a world war, the director and producers needed Spanish-looking people. So why not use Gypsies? There was a ready supply of Spanish-looking people right under their noses, and they wouldn't have to pay them. They could have their pick of thousands of Roma. These "work-shy," "racially inferior" people who had been rounded up in the last four years would provide extras for what was to be Leni Riefenstahl's masterpiece.

Django made his way to the back of the truck and squeezed in next to Lilo and her mother.

"It's going to be great, Lilo. You'll see, Frau Friwald. They have to treat us good. 'Cause we have to look good — for the cameras."

"Oh, yeah," Bluma said. "When you clean me up, I'm a regular Marlene Dietrich!" She rolled her eyes.

Lilo laughed. It was the first time her mother had made a joke since they had been arrested in Vienna. Django and Lilo continued chattering in German, rather than the dialect of either Gypsy language. Her mother used to frown at Buchenwald when she heard the Roma girls talking in their dialect. But differences tended to disappear when one stood on the brink of extinction.

KRÜN

Late Autumn 1940

Six

Lilo leaned against Django and gave him a soft jab with her elbow.

"So, big guy, you going to organize some bread for us?" The truck they were riding in took a sharp curve and lurched, so he was thrown against her. She heard a wail rise up in protest from the baby.

"Organize! Don't be ridiculous. They're going to serve us on silver platters. We're in show business now. You watch, Lilo. We have to look great for the cameras. There'll be good food, nice clothes. Leni wants us looking fantastic for the silver screen."

Django was already calling her Leni, not to her face, of course, but to the rest of the "cast." They were no longer prisoners in his mind but cast members.

Lilo looked at him out of the corner of her eye, shook her head, and laughed.

"What's so funny?"

"You, Django."

Funny was not really the right word. Django was curious more than funny. Lilo had known him only a short time—a matter of weeks. His story had come to her piecemeal—the smallest pieces imaginable—crumbs really, from his life before Maxglan, before Buchenwald, before Lackenbach, before Marzahn. But Marzahn was where Django's story really began.

Django joked about his tour of camps, and like a connoisseur of fine wines, he would expound on the subtle distinctions between a camp of concentration, a collecting-point camp, and a transit camp. But Lilo knew somehow that humor was an elaborate pretense, a masquerade that hid the horrible facts that he seldom talked about. When he did talk, it was only in the sparsest detail, as on the bus trip to Maxglan. As close as he and Lilo had become, she always sensed that there were things that had happened to him in the camps that were unspeakable.

He could name his losses: the death of a baby sister; the separation from his father and older brother; the death of his mother at Dachau, finally confirmed through some kind of concentration camp grapevine. But naming was simple; naming was not telling. She knew there were things he simply could not say. She sensed within him a deep reservoir of anger, of hatred, but with it came an unimaginable cunning and energy. It was almost as if Django did not speak of these things because to speak of them would dilute the potency of this reservoir, on which his survival depended. More than once when she had asked a question, one that cut perhaps too close to the bone, those nearly navy-blue eyes had become almost opaque and he'd snapped, "You don't need to know that," or simply, "Never mind."

"Look!" Django nudged her. They had turned off the paved road onto a dirt one that ran between two newly mown hayfields. The hay was bundled into neat little conical formations that reminded Lilo of houses that fairy folk or trolls might live in. There was a wonderful fresh smell. Ahead was a gate. A man dressed in lederhosen and a Tyrolean hat stood by to pull a rope that swung open the gate.

"Mama, cows!" Lilo exclaimed.

"And goats!" someone else said.

A silence fell on the twenty-three people as one collective vision danced in their heads. *Cheese and milk!*

The truck stopped, and the man in the lederhosen, who was obviously the farmer, came to the driver's side of the truck and began speaking and pointing. "You drive past the first house, and then there are . . ." They all fell silent trying to hear what he was saying.

"He said *first house*. So there must be a second," someone whispered.

"The farmhands' house is probably the second, but hey, it's probably empty. They've all gone to war," another person said.

Lilo thought that if all the hands had indeed gone to war, the farm looked pretty well cared for. A few minutes later, they pulled up to a large barn. A police car and SS jeep were parked in front. Half a dozen officers, either in the uniforms of the local constabulary or the tan-and-black of the SS, suddenly materialized. Two officers slid open the enormous barn door.

"Look up there, Lilo." Her mother pointed to the opening just beneath the peak of the roof, the hayloft window. Another officer stood with one foot on the edge of the opening, a rifle pointed down at them.

The back gate of the truck was opened. An officer stepped up. They were all surprised to see that it was Commandant Anton Bohmer, the head of the Maxglan camp.

"Why would he come here?" Lilo whispered to Django.

"He wants to be in movies, too."

"But if he's here . . ." The words died in Lilo's throat. *It would be just like the camp, not Hollywood.*

"Women and girls to the left, men and boys to the right."

Lilo, her mother, and ten other women and girls were led toward a long, low building with a metal roof.

"It's a milking barn," Unku said. Unku had arrived at Maxglan shortly after Lilo. She was very pretty. A few months before, Lilo's mother would have described her as "too pretty in that Roma way." But those ways of thinking were gone. She was just "fetching," as her father might have said.

"How do you know it's a milking barn?" Lilo asked.

"I worked in one once with my mother near Dusseldorf."

"They're going to give us milk!" Lilo exclaimed. Just then a woman strode up to them.

"This way, this way!" She was not in uniform but began herding them along into the barn. "Take off all your clothes. Put them in a pile. They have to be burned. Then step over by the hoses, and after that we'll give you new clothes."

The floor in the milking barn was cement, and there were two trenches separated by twenty feet. A curtain had been hung between the two trenches, and Lilo could hear the men and boys on the other side. They were being given identical instructions. "Step into the trench. Stand still. Do not leave the trench until ordered. Soap and shampoo will be issued."

Five minutes later, they were being hosed down. The water was chilly, but it still felt good.

Lilo saw the mother crouching over her infant girl to protect her from the blast of the hose. The water must have been too cold, because she was howling. *Poor thing,* Lilo thought. Then she noticed the water turning pink around her own feet. She stole a glance at her mother. She was still bleeding. But it was not the blood that shocked her. It was the knobs of her mother's pelvis jutting through skin that was thin as tissue paper. When her mother turned, she saw that her buttocks no longer had any shape at all. There was no crack, instead just a shallow gully with the skin draped over the bones. She didn't look quite human but like some sort of stick-figure construction. One might expect to see screws or bolts fastening the pieces together. Her mother shuddered as the fierce stream of the hose hit her squarely in the chest. Lilo quickly slipped her arm around her.

"Easy!" she barked at the woman with the hose and moved to protect her mother from the powerful spray of water.

"Oh, sorry, dearie. Your mum?" Lilo was stunned. No one had ever said sorry to them since before Rossauer

Lände. Not even Good Matron. She nodded. "Just a bit of a thing, ain't she? Could wash her right down the drain."

Please don't, thought Lilo.

After they had been hosed, dried, and sprayed with a disinfectant that stung, they were issued new clothes. Unku began sashaying around. "My, don't I look like a movie star in this." The clothes were the same gray coarse prison shirts and pants worn at Maxglan, only cleaner. All shirts were stamped with a Z on the front and the back. Lilo laughed at Unku's antics, but her mother scowled.

When they were dressed, they were told to stand in the paved yard outside the milk barns. Four armed guards stood watch and shortly Commandant Bohmer strode into the yard. In his hand he held a whip coiled into a perfect circle. He held it as if it were another appendage, a natural extension of his hand. He slid his fingers almost unconsciously along the leather. It was not precisely a threatening gesture. It was simply a statement, an assertion of power. He cast his eyes lazily over the twenty-three people, then tipped his head and murmured something to his aide.

"You are surprised to see me here!" He smiled. It was more of a dark gash than a facial expression. "What would you say if I told you I had a brief theatrical career? Ha! You find that funny?" Everyone knew that he did not expect an answer.

"All right, let us begin. The rules here are no different from Maxglan. There are just more. Rule number one: you are prisoners here as you were in Maxglan. When you are on the movie set, do not go near the cast and crew. Do not talk to them. There will be armed guards on the set at all times. Do not talk to the guards. If you try to escape, they will shoot you."

He continued listing the rules that they had all heard in every internment camp they had been in. He concluded by reassuring them that all infractions would be dealt with swiftly and punishments would be administered either individually or in certain cases collectively, just as at Maxglan. In other words, they could all suffer for the errors of one.

"And," he added, "if for any reason Fräulein Riefenstahl becomes dissatisfied with your work, you shall be immediately sent back to Maxglan or possibly Ravensbruck or points east." Again the gash in the face appeared.

Two young farm boys arrived; each carried two pails of milk. The prisoners were then instructed to step forward and receive their food rations.

"Here, take this, Mama." Lilo held out the metal cup of milk.

"No, no. Keep it. It's not much, anyway. Look, they watered it."

The milk had indeed been watered. But it was the best-tasting thing they had put in their mouths in months. They were also given bread and a slab of ham. Lilo sat down next to the pretty girl, Unku.

She couldn't help but reflect on how different it was to start up a conversation with a prisoner than to talk with a schoolmate. It was nothing like the first day of school, when one might ask a lot of questions about someone's hobbies or favorite sports hero or where they lived or if they had brothers, sisters. Lilo's world had shrunk so much that these questions and the information one might get would be mostly useless. Asking about family was off limits because nine out of ten times that person had lost not just one but several family members. The topics of conversation were severely limited. Lilo looked at Unku and wondered if she had been sterilized. But she dared not ask. She was surprised when Unku uttered the blunt words. "So they got your mother but not you, eh?"

"You mean . . . ?"

Unku nodded silently and inscribed a circle with her finger around her belly.

"How could you tell?"

"I saw the scars and the blood when they hosed us down."

The thing that Lilo hated most was that she was no

longer shocked. That she and Unku could talk about this seemed simultaneously unbelievable yet not shocking. A question popped into Lilo's head.

"What were you doing a year ago, this time?"

"Let's see, a year ago." Unku scratched her head. She had the most beautiful hair Lilo had ever seen. Even though her hair had been cut short, it was very thick, so thick, with glinting red highlights. Her eyes weren't black but amber. Now as she spoke, her eyes became lively with the memory of what she had been doing a year before. "Of course I remember! We were on the new winter triangle route Ostra-Brno-Zlin. It was maybe months before they passed the decree that Gypsies could no longer travel and we had to settle. We're not like you Sinti." This she didn't have to explain to Lilo. "So my grandmother is a fortune-teller, sort of."

Lilo's eyes widened. Her mother had said fortune-telling was complete nonsense. "She does the *pen dukkerin*?" Lilo asked. "Is she good?"

"Ha!" Unku laughed harshly. "We thought she was until we were caught. My grandmother was sure she could use her powers to figure out the best place to go in the triangle."

"She uses a crystal ball?"

"Only for the *gadje*." *Gadje* was the word for anyone who was not a Gypsy. It also meant dupe. Lilo knew that her mother would have been furious with her for consorting with a girl who spoke so disrespectfully, let alone a Roma girl whose grandma was a fortune-teller. But she found Unku interesting. "So what did she use instead of a crystal ball?"

"A mirrored bowl filled with water." Then Unku's eyes flashed. "Problem is, she was a lousy fortune-teller but she thought she was good."

Lilo laughed. "What, she cheated you? Pulled the *hakk'ni panki*?"

"No, instead of leading us away from the SS, she led us right to them. When we came into Brno, the SS were waiting for us. Next thing we know, we're in Lety." She sighed. "So that's what I was doing a year ago. Traveling to Lety. What were you doing?"

"Me? Oh, well, I was in school. It was recitation time. Actually no, recitation tests were usually in the late morning. It's afternoon now. Maybe mathematics. My favorite subject was history, especially ancient history — like Greece."

"Ah, you're not a caravan girl. I've never been to school. But I can read and write a little bit. And I can count. You know, add, subtract, multiply, all that."

"What did you like to do?"

"Dance!"

"I knew you were going to say that."

Unku poked Lilo with her elbow. "Ah, come on. How did you know that? You a fortune-teller like my grandmother?"

"I guessed when you were prancing around pretending to be a movie star after they gave us these clean clothes. You're very graceful. You know how to move."

"Did you have a boyfriend?" Unku suddenly asked.

"No."

"Never?"

"Well, there were boys I liked, but I wouldn't say that . . . well, you know, it never added up to anything."

"How old are you?"

"Fifteen."

"By the time I was fifteen, I had had at least seven." Unku laughed. "Close your mouth, Lilo." In fact, Lilo's mouth had dropped open in dismay. She was terribly embarrassed by her reaction and felt she must have looked completely wide-eyed, wide mouthed, and stupid.

"Well, how old are you now?" Lilo finally gathered her wits enough to ask.

"Sixteen. And don't ask how many boyfriends. I've lost count." Lilo noticed that Unku did not say this in a bragging way, and she immediately decided that she liked this Roma girl, this beautiful non-Sinti girl. She was an honest, straightforward girl. Maybe a bit rougher than the girlfriends she was accustomed to, but rough didn't mean nasty. She knew Sinti girls who could be mean as junk-yard dogs.

That night, they were locked up in the barn. Blankets had been distributed to spread on the hay. Lilo and her mother together made an "apartment" out of nine rectangular bales of hay. It seemed almost cozy. Lilo had picked a place close to the barn's east wall because there was a crack in the boards where she could look out and see the mountains and the sky.

"Mama," she whispered as they cuddled, "you see? It's going to be better here. Really. Look—we're cleaner. They gave us more to eat. You'll see, Mama. And you're bleeding less now since the shower. I can tell—you seem stronger."

"It's not quite Hollywood, though," her mother said softly. It was a joke. Her second joke in one day! Lilo took heart and held her closer, but not too tightly. She was as fragile as a bird. *Those bones. God, those bones.* She thought she could feel every one of them. Her chest was a frail cage for the beating of her heart.

Lilo looked out the crack in the barn boards. There was a half-moon, and beneath it, a star was rising. A sudden shadow sliced across the moon's light. The crack turned dark. A guard had just passed. She glimpsed his jackboots—blacker than a moonless night. But then a sharp needle of brightness. The star actually reflected for a split second in the sheen of the boots. Then it was gone.

This was better . . . better than Rossauer Lände, better than Buchenwald, better than Maxglan. For dinner, Lilo had had watered milk, a piece of good bread, a hunk of ham, and now this! Through a crack in a barn board, like dessert—a piece of the night, a bit of moon, a dab of starlight.

She was not sure what woke her up, close to dawn. Perhaps it was the emptiness in the space beside her. She panicked. Her mother was nowhere in sight. The barn door was unlocked, and she saw figures in the gray of dawn making their way toward the milking barn. She got up and wandered to the small barbed-wire enclosure outside the barn.

Lilo came across a "scene." Just as Leni Riefenstahl had done at Maxglan, Lilo raised her hand to her eye and made an O to look through. Framed in her finger viewfinder, she saw her mother crouched by a corner of the fence. She was handing a kitten through to a small child, presumably the farmer's daughter. The child must have been six or seven years old and wore a Tyrolean dirndl. A milking pail was set on the ground by her feet. She had crouched down to receive the kitten and was obviously pleased that Lilo's mother had found it. She looked up adoringly at Bluma and then leaned forward to try to kiss her through the barbed wire. But that was difficult. So she tucked the kitty into the pocket of her dirndl apron, then reached instead for Bluma's hand and pressed her mouth to it. She held it for several seconds.

Lilo liked looking at the world through her finger viewfinder. It cut out the unnecessary. It brought everything into a sharp focus despite the fact that she knew there was no magnifying lens. She felt that all her senses were heightened. The child seemed so open with Bluma. Once again the child pressed her face close to the fence and reached out with her free hand to touch her mother's cheek—a Gypsy cheek! Suddenly two guards appeared. It was the head guard, however, who bent down and shook his finger at Bluma. Lilo heard the word *verboten,* forbidden.

"But she saved my kitty," the little girl was saying.

"*Nein! Nein!* The kitty could catch a disease from these filthy Gypsies. You should be in the milking barn with your sister, helping milk the cows." The little girl looked confused. Lilo saw the younger guard glance at Bluma almost sympathetically. But again the word *verboten* cut through the dawn.

This "scene" was real, not a movie, and Lilo had learned much from it: she had learned first that the little girl was not simply innocent, but that she had a deep well of goodness in her. To her, Bluma was not a Gypsy, not a prisoner crawling with vermin, but a caring human being. She had tried to reward Lilo's mother's kindness with kindness.

Just as Django gained advantages by observing people for their likes, dislikes, strengths, and weaknesses, Lilo realized she could gain knowledge of her own. She knew that not all the guards were the same. The head guard was nothing like the young one who had accompanied him. That fellow had appeared genuinely distressed when the head guard had warned the little girl to stay away from the filthy Gypsies. He had looked with real sympathy at her mother. Lilo followed the two guards at a distance until they stopped on the far side of the fence to talk. There was a water barrel there. She crouched behind it and easily heard what they were saying.

The younger one was talking. "What happens when the weather turns? Won't they get cold in the barn?"

"Ach! They're tough, these Gypsies, Johan."

"Cold is cold, especially here in the Tyrol."

Lilo's notions about the younger guard were confirmed as she listened. And she learned his name! She was getting good at this.

"Hey, they should be happy they ain't going to the Birches. Plenty of them going to the Birches."

Birches? Lilo had no idea what they were talking about. There were certainly no birch trees around this farm. What did he mean? No time to wonder. She caught a glimpse of her mother heading back to the barn. She didn't want her to worry if she found Lilo gone. She headed back, pleased with what she had learned. It was a new curriculum and more important to her survival than learning logarithms or the history of ancient Greece.

Seven

That morning, Lilo and fifteen of the inmates were driven a short distance to the film set. She worried about leaving her mother behind. For almost four weeks, they had rarely been out of each other's sight for longer than a few minutes. Indeed the longest time was at Buchenwald, when her mother had undergone the sterilization procedure.

"It looks so real!" Unku said as a village came into view. "Small but real."

But too perfect, Lilo thought. The thatch on the roofs was so evenly trimmed, there was not a straw out of place. The shutters hung on the windows with fresh coats of paint that shined as if enameled. The stones of the well were all precisely cut. When Lilo saw a man come up to the well and easily pick up one stone and replace it with another, she realized they were not real stones at all but most likely made from papier-mâché or whatever movie people used to simulate real rocks.

The sense of unreality settled in quickly as they disembarked from the bus and soon realized that the storefronts were just that—fronts with no backs. People walked through plywood doors that opened onto nothing. The facades of the building were pieces of painted plywood propped up to render a replica of a town square. The donkeys tied to a hitching post were real. A flock of geese was herded to a coop, not by a farmer's wife but by a man in rolled-up sleeves and street pants.

"*Keine Scheisse!*" A man with a bullhorn was shouting. "Get the sweepers!"

Two young men with broad brooms materialized out of nowhere, or so it seemed to Lilo, and began sweeping up the animal droppings. Apparently the square must look perfectly clean for the opening shots. She saw a crane with a camera on it being rolled forward. On top rode a cameraman, one side of his face pressed to a long lens. He gave a jaunty thumbs-up to the bullhorn man.

"So this is Roccabruna!" Django said as they stepped off the bus.

"Is that what they call it?" Lilo asked.

"According to the script."

"Have you seen the script?"

"Bits and pieces," Django said cryptically. "I plan to organize a whole one by tonight."

Lilo looked at him and shook her head ever so slightly in wonder.

"Very Spanish, isn't it?" Django said.

"I've never been to Spain, so I couldn't tell you."

"Well, it's certainly not German."

They had been moved temporarily to an area near the tavern, which, unlike the other buildings, was not simply a front but a real space. Inside they could see tables, bunches of fake grapes hanging from hooks, wine casks, and posters of bullfighters in swinging capes. "Look, no beer steins in the tavern, no beer kegs. *Ola!*"

"*Ola?* What's that?"

"Spanish expression. They seem to say it a lot. *Ola* this, *ola* that! Just a good general all-purpose word."

"*Ola,*" Lilo repeated.

The bullhorn man was striding toward them. Was he going to give them brooms and order them to clean up as well? Lilo wondered. He stopped just short of where they were standing and looked the girls and women up and down.

"You! You! And you! And now for the fellows . . . that one over there and that one—can you hold an accordion?" He snapped his fingers at Django.

"Hold one? I can play!" Django said.

"All right, we dub in the music, but you can pretend! Look professional."

"That's me. I am the total professional!" Django brushed his shirt.

"Okay, my professional, over here!" Lilo had learned that this man was Hugo Lehner. He was one of the two men who had been at Maxglan with Fräulein Riefenstahl when she selected the prisoners.

"And the mother with baby. There's one with a baby. Right?"

The woman whom Lilo had learned was named Mina stepped forward with her swaddled infant in a sling. The baby was mewling. Mina was so thin that Lilo couldn't help but wonder how she could make enough milk for the child. Lehner walked over and pulled back the covers a bit. "Okay, good enough. Now your job is just to stand in the square near the well. That's where all the women gather—to gossip, get water, you know."

Mina nodded.

"The rest of you, wait over there until called. *Aufseher!*" He raised his hands and snapped his fingers. Two uniformed guards with pistols seemed to materialize out of nowhere.

"Escort the prisoners to the cage."

"Just like Hollywood," Lilo muttered to Rosa, another girl, who was about two years younger than she was.

In spite of not being a real village, it was nonetheless an amazing one. The real village, so to speak, the village of Krün, was next door. The cage that Lilo and the other extras were put into was near the tavern. It was more of a small corral than an actual cage. There was split-rail fencing with wire, not barbed, however, between the rails.

Lilo soon learned that there was a lot of waiting on a movie set. But for now it was exciting. She wished her mother had been brought to the set, but only fifteen had been required for the day's shooting. An assistant director came up to the corral and swung open the gate. A woman accompanied him and began picking out half a dozen girls.

"Follow me!" She waved to them. Lilo and the five others fell in line behind her. The woman had a tape measure around her neck and led them to an area at the tavern that had been roped off and draped with a cloth. It was called the costume tent and was filled with racks of clothes. She began pulling blouses and skirts from the racks. "My God, they're all so skinny. Anna, come over here. We have to start taking these in fast."

"No fat ones, Bella?" a woman asked.

"Nah. These were the healthiest I could find. You know these are the street urchins. So we can't use the older females."

Lilo's eyes widened as the woman called Anna walked up to them. She was virtually a human porcupine. Her mouth bristled with pins, and each of her wrists was encircled with a bracelet pincushion with at least one hundred pins stuck into it. On her head she wore a headband that was spiked with larger pins, mostly safety pins.

Lilo, Unku, and two other girls, Rosa and Blanca, had been given skirts and blouses that were many times too large for their thin frames. Anna and Bella, with two assistants, began to furiously sew the girls into their costumes. The stitching was not fine and tight but just basting reinforced with pins. "Just be careful how you sit," one of the assistants said. It seemed to Lilo like a strange remark at first. Except for Good Matron, no one in any camp had told them to be careful about anything that had to do with their personal well-being. But then she realized it was not really their personal well-being that was the concern but the creation of the flawless nature of the unreal world of the film.

Lilo watched as Bella and Anna put their heads together and whispered off to the side as one of the assistants worked with Unku's blouse. She found it slightly unnerving how they were looking at her so closely.

"Harald!" Bella called over to a man who was very finely dressed in riding britches. He was holding what Lilo would soon learn was the script of the film. He was tall and good-looking, and Lilo thought at first that he might be one of the actors. But she had learned that he was the assistant director and also the choreographer for Fräulein Riefenstahl's dances. He leaned over and listened intently to the two women, then looked up and fixed his gaze on Unku. Lilo felt the sharp edge of fear, like a blade scraping inside her. Why were they looking at Unku that way? Was there some problem? What could Unku have done? The man named Harald turned and walked away with a shrug, then speaking over his shoulder, said, "Well, what can we do? Do we want them all ugly? We'll see what Leni says."

"Oh, she'll say something," Bella said with a laugh. She had a deep laugh like a man's. Despite the laugh, there was something portentous in her words.

So far none of the extras had seen Leni since Maxglan. They had seen the door to her dressing room when they had come onto the set of the tavern. There was a sign, L. RIEFENSTAHL, DIRECTOR—NO ADMITTANCE. However, in the middle of the floor, where L. Riefenstahl was to dance, another woman stood in the multi-ruffled costume of a flamenco dancer.

It was strange because this woman simply stood there,

and occasionally one of the cameramen would ask her to turn this way or that. As Lilo was pondering this, Django arrived.

"She's what they call a stand-in," he explained, "someone who is about the same height, size, and coloring as the main actor and whose job is to stand in the actor's place while a shot is planned out and the lights and cameras are set up."

"How do you know all this?"

But before Django could reply to Lilo's question, another voice boomed, "Quiet, everybody. Quiet on the set, please. Fräulein Riefenstahl!"

"Hans! Hansy darling! You're going to have to raise that boom higher just a bit for the dance. You know what I want for the opening shot in this scene."

At first there was just the voice, and then out of the shadows swept a stunningly beautiful figure. She wore a long skirt with tiers of ruffles in contrasting shades of red. The blouse was a peasant style that laced up the bodice to a square neckline, and on her head she wore a mantilla. Lilo could tell it was not very good lace. Nevertheless, the entire effect was sensational. It was hard for her to believe that this was the same woman who had stepped prettily through the mud in Maxglan in her alligator boots. That woman, too, had been beautiful but not in this marvelously exotic way. No boots, no briefcase, no fine wool slacks now. She was dressed in the costume of a Spanish dancer.

The stand-in quickly receded into the shadows, and Fräulein Riefenstahl struck a pose under a beam of peach-colored light. "Steeper," she called out. "I want steeper angles for both cameras. Not higher but steeper. Understand? And the lighting from below washes up — low lighting but luminous on the cheekbones." She framed her cheek with her hands in a self-caressing gesture. "Then you get this! It's that Gypsy light. That's what I want — that Gypsy light, I call it. Got it, Alberto?"

"Yes!" a voice emanated from the darkness. Above, in the folds of shadows, a cameraman was riding on the boom.

"Music!" someone called out.

The music was from a recording, but a guitarist sat at the edge of the dance area, pretending to strum.

Lilo observed Django making a face as if to say, "You call that playing?"

Her mother had told her that Leni Riefenstahl began her career as a dancer. But there was something peculiar in the way she moved. Possibly it was the bad music. It seemed exaggerated, every movement a bit overdone, almost drastic, Lilo thought.

She lost track of the number of takes for the scene. Perhaps a dozen until they got it the way Fräulein

Riefenstahl wanted it. At the finish, the extras were told to report to another station in the tavern that had been roped off. There were several chairs and some standing mirrors.

"This must be the makeup department," Lilo whispered to Blanca. "If our mothers could see us now. Sinti girls getting rouged up like Roma tarts!" They both giggled.

Unku was already seated. The makeup technician was a round little woman whose dyed red hair was twisted into an elaborate knot that perched on top of her head like a miniature sultan's turban. She was exclaiming over Unku's complexion. "Skin like a Gypsy angel. That rose flush beneath the copper hue! *Mein Gott,* and those lashes. Hardly anything I need to do."

"Tone her down, Janni!" Anna had just come up to the chair where Unku sat.

Then suddenly the man called Harald came up to Anna and she gave him a peck on the cheek. They put their heads together and whispered for a moment while looking at Lilo and the other girls who had been herded into makeup. Mostly they were younger prisoners, under twenty. The small boy who had stood next to Django in the line at Maxglan when Leni had first selected them as extras was there. He was no more than seven or eight and was dressed with a white apron tucked around his waist.

He was to be a waiter in the tavern. Leni asked for a tray and a jug of wine and made her way toward him.

"*Liebling,* what's your name?"

"Otto," the boy replied.

"Otto? It doesn't sound like a Gypsy name."

"Neither does Martha," the man named Harald said. "You know what Arnold thinks."

"I don't give a goddamn what Arnold thinks. He's not here. I fired him."

Django had made his way to Lilo's side. "Martha is the name of the Spanish dancer in the script," he whispered.

"How do you know?" Lilo asked, and once again, for perhaps the one hundredth time since she had first met Django, wondered how he acquired such massive amounts of information when the rest of them knew nothing.

"I'll tell you later."

"And who's Arnold?"

"Arnold Fanck—the most famous director in Germany . . . well, almost, after von Sternberg—*Blue Angel,* you know, Marlene Dietrich."

"Yes, I know about *The Blue Angel,* but this Arnold, why did she fire him?"

Django shrugged. "Who's to know? But she really hates him. I heard some of the crew talking about it."

Django moved off to where the boy extras were being assembled. He was barefoot, dressed in rags, and his legs were covered with soot. It wasn't quite the costume he had envisioned. What Lilo was wearing was clean but had been artistically ripped, and smudges of dirt had been applied to her cheeks.

Now Leni, after giving Otto a lesson on how to carry a tray with a wine bottle, was making her way toward Lilo and the other girls. She smiled. Although she was breathtakingly gorgeous, Lilo found something alarming about her beauty. Then after perhaps a minute of watching her talk, she realized it was those close-set eyes. They suffused the beauty of her face with a feral light. Lilo could imagine her sniffing—sniffing out prey with that sharp nose. It was not hard to visualize the nostrils quivering as she picked up a new scent. There was something brutal about her face. She had heard that some Nazis claimed they could smell the inferior races—Jews or Gypsies or Negroes. Was she one who thought she could do that?

Fräulein Riefenstahl addressed the girls now, the street urchins. "My darlings, you must all call me Tante Leni. We are going to have so much fun." The words sent a shiver through Lilo. *I don't want to have fun with this woman,* she thought. Fräulein Riefenstahl dipped her hand into a pocket. "I have brought some chocolate for each of you." She began distributing candies wrapped in silver and gold foil.

Lilo thought now not of the gingerbread man but of the gingerbread house, deep in the dark woods, and of the old crone who lured Hansel and Gretel inside with palmfuls of candy.

"Chocolate!" Blanca sighed. Chocolate was an ancient, nay, an almost prehistoric, memory for all of them.

Fräulein Riefenstahl moved down the line of street urchins, offering them the foil-wrapped candy.

"Go on. Take it, *Liebling*," she said when Lilo hesitated, merely staring at the extended palm. It was as if her own hand had frozen by her side.

"Don't like chocolate?" Lilo said nothing. "Come on!" An impatient rasp edged her voice. *If I take it, I die.* That was all Lilo could think. Was it like the candy house that had lured Hansel and Gretel?

"We gotta stubborn one here?" The elegant woman steeped in ruffles suddenly seemed quite vulgar. Lilo reached out and took the chocolate. The brutal eyes drew a bead on her, and Lilo felt as if she were caught in the thin crosshairs of a rifle's sights. "That's a nice girl," Leni said, and reached out and lightly touched Lilo's cheek. In that split second, Lilo felt as if she had been branded. *God, never let her touch my skin again.*

Lilo stared at the chocolate. It had been so long! Suddenly she could hardly resist tearing the foil right off. *But I must eat only half. Can I eat only half? And save the other for Mama?* But if she ate it, what did it mean? What kind of devil had she and the other children struck a bargain with? How had Lilo and her mother ever even in jest said that this was her father's girlfriend? If only her father could see this woman up close as she had, he would know . . . *Know what?* Lilo thought. Know that she was a predator and was feared as much as any wolf.

She had moved on, and Lilo felt only relief.

"Who's this?" It was like a razor strop cutting the air. Lilo jerked her attention from the golden-foil-wrapped nugget. Leni was standing before Unku. Even though Unku was dressed in rags and had streaks of dirt on her face, her beauty shined through.

An assistant with a clipboard rushed over and shuffled through papers. "Uh, this is, let's see . . . this is Unku Graff."

"How old are you?"

"Sixteen," Unku whispered.

Lilo, even standing three feet away, felt Unku's terror.

"Better a whore, I think, than an urchin," Leni said softly.

"Leni, we need urchins following you around, not whores. You are the idol of the village children." Harald had come up to her and put his arm around her shoulders. She shook him off.

"Well, make her look younger. Call the hairdresser.

Much too much hair. Cut it. It will make her look younger, and sew up the blouse. We don't need to see her tits."

From her pocket, she drew out not a chocolate but a small notebook. It was the same notebook Lilo had seen her write in at Maxglan. She now wrote something down in it. When she had finished writing, she looked around at the street urchins, who were all watching her. She smiled slightly, then looked down and wrote something else, closed the notebook, and tucked it into her pocket. The entire operation took no more than thirty seconds, but it was as choreographed as the dance she had performed for the camera.

Eight

"Mama, can you carry a jug on your head?"

"What do you think I am, a peasant?" Bluma was sitting in the barn, playing with one of the barn cat's kittens.

"Mama!" Lilo rolled her eyes. "It's only acting."

"Why would I want to act like a peasant? I am a lace maker."

Please, please, Lilo prayed silently. *Don't be stubborn, Mama.* "Mama, let me explain this carefully." She crouched down and picked up the kitty, then looked right into her mother's eyes. "Django says —"

"Django says." Her mother spoke scornfully. "Django says this. Django says that. You believe everything that boy says." Lilo felt a mixture of embarrassment and anger.

"No, not really. I can think for myself. So forget what Django says, then. But I do know that if you don't work here, if they can't find a part for you as an extra, you go back." She let the words sink in. They caught Bluma's attention. "Back to Maxglan, or east, Mama," she whispered.

Bluma rose slowly. There was an empty bucket nearby. She bent over and picked it up. She put it on her head and walked three steps. "If I can walk with a bucket on my head, I can walk with a jug. Of course, silly girl."

Lilo clapped her hands. "Oh, Mama!" She squealed happily.

Bluma took the bucket off just as Unku walked by.

"What happened to you?" Bluma asked. But Unku kept walking sullenly and did not answer. "What happened to her, Lilo?" Bluma whispered.

"Fräulein Riefenstahl made the hairdressers chop off most of her hair to make her look younger."

"Heh!" This was the distinctive snort her mother gave when she was scornful of something.

"Younger? She just didn't want anyone prettier. The woman is vain. And what's more, she's dangerous. I saw it from the first step she took through the mud at Maxglan. I know vain women. Remember, I work in fashion. Unku was too pretty." She paused. "And you know what else?"

"What else, Mama?"

"This isn't Hollywood, and we're not extras. They lock the barn, remember? We bathe in the cow barn and go to latrines. We sit on rough boards to do our business. You think Gary Cooper did this or Marlene Dietrich when they were making *Morocco*? We're film slaves." She paused, and her face became still. "But I'll carry the jug."

Lilo knew that her mother was right. She was a quick study. She hadn't seen Leni Riefenstahl for more than a couple of minutes back at Maxglan, but she had summed her up. Her body might be failing, but Bluma Friwald's mind was sharp as ever. Lilo found this heartening.

"You be careful of that woman, Lilo. She cut the pretty Roma girl's hair. She could do a lot worse, I bet."

Lilo thought of the notebook but decided not to tell her mother.

"Don't worry, Mama. I'm not pretty enough."

Bluma looked at her daughter with an inscrutable expression clouding her eyes. She pressed her mouth together, and the corners tipped down. Her mother almost never cried, but she looked like she was about to now. Why was she looking at her in this way? What did she see? Lilo always knew she wasn't ugly, but she had just missed being pretty. Her nose was too long, her eyes too big for her narrow face. Her chin sharp and her eyebrows so thick they reminded her of woolly caterpillars. Her hair had never been as lustrous and thick as Unku's, and now an ugly reddish cast had crept into it, which her mother had told her came from hunger and no decent food. Indeed she had noticed it in some other prisoners' hair.

At that moment, Django came along. Bluma put the bucket back on her head. "Will this do, Django?"

His face lit up. "It certainly will, Frau Friwald!" He held a thick packet in his hand. It was the shooting script for the film. He had "organized" it.

That evening over a bowl of potato soup, which actually had some meat in it, Django and Lilo and Rosa studied the shooting script. Not of course before Django launched into how terrible the music was in the tavern scene.

"It was a record they were playing, not live music. The guitarist just had to fake the fingering," Lilo said. "I saw it, behind a curtain."

"His fingering was all wrong, and the music they chose was ridiculous. They should have me holding the guitar and not the accordion. Besides, I wasn't in one shot with the stupid accordion. I could show them a thing or two about real Spanish music," Django said. It was one of the few times Lilo had ever heard him really angry.

"Enough of your music review. Tell us about the film. What's the script like?" Rosa said, tucking a short strand of hair behind her ear. Lilo flinched when she saw some of the hair simply fall out, but Rosa didn't seem to notice.

She had once been a very pretty girl. She had a straight little nose and high cheekbones and blue eyes.

"First off, I discovered that this film is not just *one* of the most expensive but *the* most expensive film ever to be made in Germany. I heard them talking. She—Tante Leni—"

"Are we really going to call her that?" Rosa asked.

"I don't think we have a choice," Lilo replied, and fingered her chocolate, which she had somehow resisted eating and planned to share with her mother before bed.

"She was given fifty thousand reichsmarks for just this part here in Krün, and it's only, as they say, the tip of the iceberg," Django said.

"Who's paying for this?" Lilo asked.

He opened the script to the inside cover. "See that stamp?" The girls bent close to look at it.

"The Reich Film Department," Rosa whispered.

"Yes, Hitler, the Third Reich, is footing the bill here."

Lilo and Rosa both sat back. It all seemed very confusing.

"Why should the government pay for it?" Lilo asked.

Django sighed. "She's a charmer, that one. She's obviously charmed the Führer."

All Lilo could think of when Django said the word *charmer* was *snake*. Tante Leni was both the snake and the charmer. In her mind's eye, she saw Fräulein Riefenstahl writhing up from a conjurer's basket with her glittering beady eyes.

"What do you think that notebook is that she always carries?" Lilo asked.

Django shrugged. For once he didn't have an answer.

"Django, tell us the story of the movie," Rosa said.

"All right. The scenes with the red marks by them have already been shot, and you can see that they don't go in order at all. They haven't even filmed the opening scene. They have to go to the Dolomites for that. The hero, Pedro, kills a wolf."

"A wolf!" Lilo exclaimed.

"Yeah, a wolf. What's wrong with that?"

"Nothing . . . nothing at all," Lilo said. "Go on."

"The wolf is threatening the shepherd's flock of sheep — well, actually they're the marquis's sheep. The shepherd works for the nobleman. And there's a knife scene toward the end where Pedro kills the marquis."

Rosa laughed. "Oh, thanks for spoiling the ending for us."

"I'm confused," Lilo said. "The ending can't spoil anything if you don't know the story. Tell us the story. And begin at the beginning. Why are they calling it *Tiefland*?"

"All right. Here it is: First, *Tiefland* means lowlands. There are problems in Roccabruna, which is in the lowlands. There's not enough water. The greedy marquis,

Don Sebastian, owns prize bulls. He gets the stream diverted so he can water his bulls. The farmers, therefore, don't have enough water. No water means no crops. And no crops means no money. Farmers can't pay the rent to their lord and master, Don Sebastian. Pedro is a shepherd for the Don's goats or sheep or whatever grazes up there. Now, you have to understand that lowlands doesn't just mean low in the geographic way. No, it's a symbol." He pulled his mouth down in a sarcastic grimace. "This is fancy literature, I guess. It means low-down, bad people. And in case the audience misses the symbolism, someone warns Pedro, "Don't go to the lowlands, Pedro. The devil lives there."

"Okay, we get it," Rosa said. "On with the plot."

"I know what's going to happen, Django doesn't need to tell us," Lilo said confidently while scraping up the last dregs from the soup bowl with her fingers. "Pedro and Don Sebastian both fall in love with Martha. Pedro wins. The good guy always wins. That's what happens in the end with the knife fight, right?" Everyone fell silent as soon as Lilo said this. But now she felt foolish, because she knew that it was not that the script was so simple but that life was more complicated.

The good guys didn't always win. Django, Rosa, Lilo, and Bluma had lost in every battle so far. This was proof enough that the bad guys had already won over and over again. When there were no more people to be killed, maybe that's when Hitler would lose.

Django broke the silence. "Yeah. You've got it, Lilo. Simple." That one word cut deeply. It was the only time he had ever betrayed any contempt. That she should have provoked it felt horrible.

She sighed. "How's Unku doing?"

Both Rosa and Django shrugged.

"I think I'll go see her," she said suddenly, and jumped up to leave. Django reached out and brushed her hand softly. He was saying he was sorry—she knew it. Her eyes filled, but she was still ashamed.

"Unku?" she called softly when she reached the top rung of the ladder to the hayloft where Unku slept. "Unku?"

"Yeah?"

"It's me, Lilo." She scrambled up over to the loft window, where Unku had made her pallet with the blankets.

"Don't say it doesn't look so bad, please."

"It looks terrible."

Unku laughed. "Good, at least you're honest." She raised her hand to her head and rubbed it. "Look—I even have a bald patch." She tipped her head forward, and indeed, there was a spot the size of a five-reichsmark coin.

"They made that with scissors?"

"Oh, no. Fräulein Riefenstahl herself took the razor and very carefully shaved that." Unku paused. "She's very careful about details." There was something in the way Unku said these last words that made Lilo's heart almost stop.

"Details," she whispered.

"Yes, details. Did you see that notebook she took out and wrote in?"

"Yes," Lilo said.

"Did you wonder what she wrote down?"

"Sort of?" Lilo lied.

"I think she wrote something about me. She took it out again just after she cut my hair, and asked my name again."

"She did?"

Unku nodded solemnly, tears beginning to run down her cheeks.

Lilo didn't know what to say. "Unku, your hair will grow back." As soon as the words were out, she knew it was the stupidest thing in the world to say.

Unku looked at her. Her eyes were seething with anger now and not tears. "It's not my hair, you fool! It's everything. My mama, my papa, my older sister, my only brother. I can't grow *them* back again. They take everything! Everything, Lilo. Even your mother's insides."

• • •

Lilo was not sure how long she had been sleeping when she heard a whimpering in the night. She opened her eyes and listened carefully. It wasn't Unku. It sounded too young, but not a baby. Or rather not the baby—the little girl who had cried most of the night before but had at last gone to sleep this evening. A child? She got up from the hay and went to investigate.

At first she thought it was just a pile of dirty old blankets stuffed in what looked like a feeding trough, but as she approached, she saw something stir under the blankets. Bending over, she lifted a corner of the coverings. It was the small boy, Otto. He was sobbing in his sleep. She put a hand on his heaving shoulder and patted him gently. This seemed to wake him.

"Bad dream?" she asked.

"Oh, no. Good dream about my mother." He rubbed his eyes, looked at her, and then sat up in the trough. He was so small. Probably not bigger than the calves or lambs that might eat from the trough. He looked around. "This is the bad dream," he said.

She looked at him. What was it about the youngest boys that they all looked like little old men—wizened before their time?

"Your name is Otto, right?"

He nodded. "Otto Kunz. My mother is Frieda Kunz."

He paused and then added in a barely audible whisper, "But she's not here."

"Do you know where she is?" Lilo asked.

He shook his head mournfully. The gesture was so slight, so slow, it was as if this small movement caused him profound pain.

"I have to go to the bathroom," he said finally.

"I'll have the guards unlock the door and take you."

"Can you take me to the ladies'? I don't like to go to the men's latrine. Sometimes the guards are there late at night." Again he paused, then added, "They scare me, especially the head guard."

"He scares me, too."

The boy looked up at her and smiled, then took her hand and gave it a squeeze as he stepped from the trough.

Nine

There must be some mistake," Django was saying to the bus driver. "Bluma Friwald is on the list, I am sure. They are shooting scene six, right?"

"Right," said the bus driver, consulting his clipboard.

"And it calls for twelve older peasant women in the square when Pedro arrives."

"Yes, indeed."

"Well, one of those women is to be Bluma Friwald. I heard Fräulein Riefenstahl specifically say yesterday to bring a tall one for the shot by the village gates. See if they added her name down here someplace." Then very politely Django asked. "May I look at your clipboard?" The driver handed it to him. "Ah, right here. Bluma Friwald." Django pointed with his finger to a place on the paper.

The bus driver nodded. Then he said almost cheer-fully, "Well, if Fräulein Riefenstahl wants a tall one — yes, I guess she is in comparison to the others. Bring her along. Can't hurt."

"Thank you, old man." Django gave the bus driver a friendly pat on the shoulder, indeed the kind of pat one old man might give another old man.

Lilo had watched this entire performance hardly dar-ing to breathe. So much depended on it. How had he done it? He was incredible. Could she have done that? Had she missed some opportunity to help her mother? She had a lot to learn from Django, but she felt for the first time stirrings of other feelings, feelings that had very little to do with what she could merely "learn" from him. She shouldn't let other feelings about him get in the way. She thought she had been smart when she had ascertained that the guard named Johan was sympathetic as opposed to the head guard. But that was nothing compared to the infor-mation that Django was able to collect. Compared to this! He had made a study not just of the guards but also of the entire film crew, right down to this bus driver, apparently. He knew who was bribable and who was not. Who was stupid and who was smart. He had told Lilo that in camps, he was quick to learn which *Kapos* and guards were really vicious.

"You must become invisible for those," he had told

her. "They are worse than animals." How do you become invisible? Lilo had asked. "It's a skill. You find shadows to stand in during roll calls. You look like this." Suddenly the light drained out of his eyes. They became dead, as if he had no more life than a stone. There was nothing there. Then quickly he came back to life. "See? What fun is it killing something that's already dead?"

Lilo knew that she had to stop being simply in awe of Django and start really learning from him. He had already figured out that the bus driver was less than swift.

When they got on the bus, Lilo sat next to him. "How did you do that? My mother's name couldn't be on the list."

"It's not. The fellow can't read."

"But how did you know that?"

"I had a hunch he was sort of dumb. I sat right behind him yesterday when we were driving to the set. I saw him struggling to read a newspaper headline. He was try- ing to sound out the first word in the headline. He couldn't do it and threw the paper down on the floor of the bus. He didn't want to admit he couldn't read—to a Gypsy, no less. He saved face by pretending when I pointed to a name."

"But Django, her name isn't on the list, and what if they discover this when we get there? We'll all be in trouble."

"Don't worry. We'll cross that bridge when we come

to it. And her name will be on the list by tomorrow. I guarantee it. There's more to worry about with Unku. Believe me."

"Yes," Lilo said softly. Unku sat a few rows ahead. Lilo could see her bald spot quite clearly. Her eyes fastened on it. *What an ogre this Leni Riefenstahl is. How low will she stoop?*

Twenty minutes later, the bus rolled up and stopped in front of the fake village of Roccabruna.

"Good heavens," Bluma gasped. "They built a whole village for this movie."

"Yes. I told you."

"But I never imagined."

"Well, some of the buildings are just fronts. You know, flats, like on a stage."

"If only it were all just a stage." Bluma sighed and stepped off the bus. She didn't have to explain. Lilo instantly understood. Yes, how lovely if Buchenwald had been just a stage or Rossauer Lände and wherever they had taken her father.

They hadn't walked far from the bus when Lilo spotted the most handsome man she had ever seen in her life standing by the tavern. He was tall and lean, deeply tanned with wavy blond hair, and even from where she stood, she could see that his eyes matched the sky. A bit of golden hair curled out from the deep V of his shepherd's shirt.

She felt herself blush. How stupid of her. He could be a Nazi. *Could be? Probably is,* she thought. *And most likely if he sees me, he thinks of vermin. Dirty Gypsy girl.*

"Your typical Spaniard, right?" Django whispered in Lilo's ear.

"Huh?"

"Pedro. Franz Eichberger."

"Pedro? The shepherd? That's him? You gotta be crazy."

"No, not me. Fräulein Riefenstahl. She's crazy for him."

Franz Eichberger strode around the set like a golden god who had just descended from the loftiest peaks of Mount Olympus. His teeth sparkled, his eyes twinkled, and his hair shimmered like curly licks of yellow flame. Lilo thought he was so beautiful that it almost hurt to look at him, like looking directly at the sun on the brightest day — one needed dark glasses.

"My God, he's handsome. Hard to believe he's mortal. Does he eat? Talk?" Lilo asked Rosa, who was standing next to Django.

"Does he take a crap?" Django laughed and looked at the two awestruck girls.

"Don't!" Lilo jabbed him with her elbow but couldn't help laughing. "But look at him. He's at least twenty years younger than Fräulein Riefenstahl."

"Almost. She's forty. He's twenty-three," Django said.

"How do you know that?" Rosa asked.

"I picked up the newspaper the bus driver threw away. It was a local paper and had stuff about shooting the movie here."

"What else did you learn about him?"

"He's a ski instructor. You know, like so many shepherds, they teach skiing on the side. Very popular profession. She discovered him on the slopes of St. Anton."

"No! Don't kid with me."

"I'm not. He was actually on active military duty. He was a ski instructor for the *Wehrmacht* in the Alps."

"The Nazi army?" Lilo sighed.

"That *Wehrmacht*—what else? The ski division. It's just being formed really, the *Skijäger*. They're being trained to use skis for movement during the winter, especially if action opens up on the eastern front."

"You mean Russia?" Lilo asked.

"Yes, now, which would you rather do if you were a man—ski to Russia in the dead of winter or be in the sack with Leni Riefenstahl?"

"Ski to Russia! Safer, I think," she said, and walked away to the area that had been roped off for them. The Gypsy extras were the only ones on the set whose movements were confined. It was the same as when they were shooting in the tavern the day before.

The outside area where they were enclosed now was right next to a corral where the animals for the movie were kept. There were several horses, dogs, five or six burros, and the flock of geese. Lilo didn't mind it. She liked the smell of the manure, the straw. It reminded her of Piber, Uncle Andreas, and the splendid Lipizzaner Cosmos. But at the same time, it made her sad. As soon as the war broke out the horses from Piber had all been sent to Czechoslovakia to protect the breed. And God knew where Uncle Andreas had been sent.

These horses, of course, could not compare to the ones in Piber. These were very skinny, like the Gypsy extras, with scruffy coats. But it was not just that. Had they been fat with gleaming coats, they would still never have been the equals of a Lipizzaner. The Lipizzaners' hooves, oddly enough, were tiny and seemed as delicate as a ballerina's feet. Despite their rather long backs, the Lipizzaners were compact, very muscular, with a deep, wide chest. Uncle Andreas had told Lilo that their chests were where their power came from. It was those chests that held the huge lungs that gave them blasts of oxygen so they could do amazing things like jump straight up high into the air with all four legs off the ground at once. Uncle Andreas's joke had been that they could do the airs because they had so much air! Her mind went back to those magical summer days.

It seemed unbelievable to Lilo that a scant four months ago she had been in Piber, riding in the instruction ring and just beginning to learn "the airs." As her uncle had explained, the airs might seem silly in the twentieth century. But there was a practical reason for them in olden days, when battles were fought on horseback. They allowed the rider, when surrounded by the enemy, to almost magically escape with moves like the capriole, in which the horse jumps straight up into the air while kicking out with its hind legs.

Her uncle Andreas in his summer livery, the gray fitted coat and darker gray jodhpurs, stood in the center of the ring with his white training whip. The whip, with its long tail, never touched the horses but was employed more like the baton of a conductor leading an orchestra. Holding the whip high over his head, Uncle Andreas would flick it. The long tail would unfurl, tracing a pattern against the sky. The crack of the whip was a cue for both the horse and the rider as to which movement was expected. Automatically, or almost automatically, Lilo would know to squeeze her knees or dig in her heels to the horse's flanks, or perhaps shift her weight slightly in the saddle. Very few words were ever spoken. There was instead a profound silence punctuated only by the sound of the whip, the breathing of the horse, and the very light impact of the hooves in the tanbark. Occasionally a breeze would blow across the surrounding meadows, bringing the whinnies of grazing horses and the sweet fragrance of grass.

As Lilo watched these horses on the set, she thought that with their big old cloppers, narrow chests, and withered rumps, they couldn't have been more opposite from the beautiful horses of Piber. Indeed they looked as if they might break under the weight of a rider.

"Stop looking at the horses." Django came up and put a hand gently on her lower back. She closed her eyes for a second as a deep thrill ran through her from Django's touch. "Look over there."

"Where?"

"Look at your mother."

"Mama!" She suddenly panicked. Had they discovered Django's shenanigans?

"Look, she's the lead peasant lady." Lilo jumped up. There was her mother, dressed in black with a head scarf and a clay water jug on her head. She was standing by the stone arch that led into the village. Harald, the assistant director, was waving his arms at the man who was operating the camera on the end of a long boom. There was another camera on a small cart that ran on a track. "That's for a dolly shot," Django said.

"What's a dolly shot? But wait—that's not Pedro. That man's . . . ugly!"

"That's Pedro's stand-in. They don't want the star

to tire himself out, you know. There's Leni—see her?" Django pointed.

Leni, dressed in some sort of robe, not a costume, was holding a device up to her eye. "What's she doing with that thing? Is it a camera?" Lilo asked.

"No. Just a viewfinder lens. Better than fingers for framing the shot. You know, cuts everything out except what she wants in the frame."

"Just like at Maxglan."

"Yes, and luckily we didn't get cut out!"

Luckily. But how long will luck last? She thought of that notebook. The one Unku had said her name was now written in. Lilo had seen Tante Leni draw the notebook out twice already this morning. She seemed to do it when she was standing near the extras. But now she had dropped the viewfinder and was forming the **O** again with her fingers to look at something else on the set. Lilo caught her breath as she saw Leni swing the **O** toward her. Once again she had that feeling of being caught in the crosshairs of a rifle's sights. Would she next pull out the notebook?

Suddenly Harald cried out *"Ruhe am das Bühnenbild!"*— Quiet on the set! They all fell silent. "Action!"

The ugly stand-in had vanished, and Pedro strode through the archway. His broad sombrero was tipped back so a few of his golden curls were visible. He had a rather bland smile on his face. Lilo immediately sensed that

Franz Eichberger was not the world's greatest actor. *No Gary Cooper,* she thought. Lilo and her mother had seen Cooper in *Morocco.* How they loved that movie! And it was while she was looking at Pedro walk through the gate for the fifth take, not a foot from where her mother stood with a jug on her head, that the truth of her mother's words struck her. *Film slaves! We are truly slaves!*

The crew and the actors had taken a break for lunch. They sat at a long table under the shade of a linden tree. The table was spread with all sorts of delectable foods, foods Lilo hadn't seen for weeks, like oranges and a platter of sliced tomatoes. There was also the smell of a fresh noodle pudding. She watched as a woman in a white apron trimmed with a ruffle delivered a tiered platter of delicate little cakes just like the kind they displayed in the window of the Fritzlmeyer Conditori shop on Maria-Theresein Strasse. And from the shadows of their enclosure, Lilo watched as Tante Leni peeled her orange very slowly and then fed a section of it to Franz, letting her fingers linger on the edge of his lips.

Their own food was delivered as well—in buckets. They were given the same tin bowls as the day before, and it was the same soup as well. Undoubtedly, it was superior to the food they had received at Rossauer Lände,

Buchenwald, or Maxglan. Still, it had more potato peel than actual potato. But as Bluma always said, the peel had all the vitamins. There was a little bit of ham in it, and they were given a decent hunk of not-too-stale bread.

Lilo still had the chocolate in her pocket. She had offered it to her mother, but Bluma had refused, saying it was too rich to eat after all these weeks. She knew it would make her sick to her stomach. Lilo had been very tempted to eat it and was not worried about becoming ill, yet every time, she stopped just short of unwrapping the gold foil that enclosed the luscious treat. The chocolate brought the image of the snake charmer and the snake to mind. That very white palm that had extended toward her with the chocolate, waiting for her to take it, reminded her of the diamond-shaped head of a cobra about to rear.

She smelled the chocolate when the other kids unwrapped theirs. Some had a cherry in the middle, some a praline or chestnut filling. She knew that she might never find out what filled her chocolate. It seemed to her that it was all part of the predator's game. The baited trap. It was Lilo's subtle stand against this insidious enemy. She was convinced that there was a profound evil lurking beneath the flawlessly beautiful surface.

Leni was walking toward them with a big smile. Some of the younger kids jumped to their feet. *"Guten Tag,* Tante

Leni." She stopped at the fence and smiled broadly. Her teeth were very white and slightly pointed. She reached her hand into the robe pocket and came out with a fistful of chocolates.

"Hooray!" the children shouted, and crowded toward the chicken-wire fence.

"Now, darlings," she said as her eyes were scanning the enclosure. Lilo knew instantly she was searching for Unku. "I want to tell you about the scene we shall be shooting this afternoon. You of course know that we often do things a bit out of order in a movie. So you have already seen me performing the dance — you watched through the tavern window. But now we are doing the scene that would occur just before the dance scene. The scene of me preparing for my first performance in the tavern, tying my dancing shoes, fixing my earrings. You children have been following me through the streets and gather outside where I am getting ready. You are peeking in at me through the opening of my caravan. Won't it be fun? All right?"

"Always peeking through windows, admiring her," Rosa whispered to Lilo.

"All right," they all cried. Tante Leni's eyes flashed, and she slid them toward Lilo as if seeking her out especially.

"Yes!" Lilo cried, and dragged her mouth into a broad smile. Was it a game they were playing? Had Tante Leni marked her in the notebook as the girl reluctant to take the chocolate? Suddenly the chocolate seemed like dead weight in her pocket.

"I think for this scene we need only girls," Leni continued. "No boys and preferably the shorter girls. Maybe one medium-tall girl. Like you." She pointed directly at Lilo. She paused and looked toward Unku, who was taller. "That one in the back. Why don't we dress her in the long black skirt and black scarf? She can be standing by the well with some of the other village crones. Oh, and where is that mother with the baby, Harald?"

"In the holding cage, I believe." Harald had just come up.

"Well, get her. I think it would be adorable if she could hold the baby up to the window to give the infant a peek at me as well."

"I think the mother is nursing the baby."

"Well, she could take it off her tit for a moment, for God's sake. I think it would be charming if she held it up to the window. Don't you, Harald?" The dark beady eyes bore into him. He shrugged.

"Of course, Leni—charming, adorable," he muttered.

Two minutes later, Harald was back with the mother and baby. Leni came up to them. The baby was fussing a bit. "May I peek?" she said in a soft voice.

"Of course," the mother replied.

"Oh, he's adorable."

"It's a girl, madam."

"Oh, sorry." Leni tossed her head coquettishly. "She's adorable. She'll grow up to be a real beauty, I am sure."

The scene in the square was shot quickly, but then it was decided that the tavern scene that they had worked on a few days before had some lighting problems and had to be reshot. The street urchins were back outside the tavern, peeking in at the Martha dance. Nothing seemed to be going right in the scene, and tempers were fraying.

"Look at that!" Rosa whispered between takes.

"What?" Lilo said.

"Tante Leni—shaking her finger at little Otto." He was trying his best not to burst into sobs. The child was not more than ten feet away from the window where Lilo, Rosa, and Blanca were standing.

"He's tired, Leni." Harald Reinl strode over. "Give the kid a break."

"Give him a break? This isn't my money. It's the Reich's."

"He's carried that tray perfectly for what, twenty-five takes now?"

Then Lilo and Rosa stared at each other as the child fell down on his knees. "I want my mother, Tante Leni."

"Being tired is not the problem, apparently," Leni said.

Leni stooped down, the ruffles of her skirt nearly

swamping the child. They could see her extending her hand and stroking Otto's curly black hair—a wig, which covered his closely shaved head. But now he tore off the wig and shouted "No!" directly at Tante Leni, who held out chocolates to him. "You promised me before. No! No! No! I want my mother. I don't want chocolates."

Leni turned and snapped her fingers. The lady who was in charge of dressing Leni came forward and handed her the small notebook. "You already wrote her name down in the notebook. Frieda Kunz!" Otto cried.

"You are right. I am not writing down her name. How do we find your mama if I don't know your name, *Liebling*." There was something in the way she said "mama" that made Lilo's stomach curdle.

As if in a trance, the child replied, "My name is Otto Anton Kunz."

From the basket of red ruffles that surrounded him, he tipped up his face to Tante Leni and took a deep breath. "Please, I want my mother. Her name is Frieda Kunz. She is a tall lady. She has a dimple when she smiles. She speaks Sinti and Roma and Italian, and she sings beautifully. Please find her, Tante Leni."

"Of course, *Liebling*. Now, you run along. Are you sure you don't want a chocolate?"

Take it! Take it, Lilo prayed.

"No, thank you. All I want is Mama."

Ten

"Where is he?" Rosa whispered as they got off the bus at the farm.

"I thought he came on the first bus," Blanca said.

"Django was on the first bus." Lilo looked around for Django and spotted him by a newly erected fence.

The head guard greeted them.

"Welcome back. The farmer Herr Cramm has been kind enough to enlarge the fenced area significantly so that you may take a moderate amount of exercise outside the barn." He looked at Lilo and the others as if he expected to be thanked. Then he briskly nodded and walked away. Lilo, Rosa, and Blanca raced over to Django.

"Was Otto on your bus?" Lilo asked.

"Little Otto? No, why?"

"Oh, God—she took him!" Lilo gasped.

"More likely sent him away," Rosa added.

"Maybe she really did send him to meet his mother," Lilo said.

The color drained from Django's face. "His mother? Otto's mother is at Dachau."

"B-b-but that's not like those horrible camps that we hear are being built in the east," Lilo stammered.

"Until those camps are completed in Poland. It's a major holding camp until then. Like Buchenwald."

"But how do you know, Django?" Rose asked. "You can't be sure."

"I was in Marzahn with Frieda Kunz. She was sent to Dachau. Otto was put on the bus with me to Buchenwald. I looked after him. All the Gypsies from Marzahn who were shipped to Dachau are heading east now."

"But how do you know for sure?" Lilo pressed. Django's eyes shifted nervously.

"The guard Gunther." He nodded toward the head guard, who had just informed them of the farmer's largesse in building the fence. "I heard him talking the other night. Auschwitz is almost completed. Gypsies and Jews are being sent by the thousands to finish the construction—in short, to dig their own graves, in the Birches."

"The birches?" Lilo was stunned. *They should be glad they aren't being sent to the birches.* The head guard's words came back to her from the first chilly night nearly a month before. "What are the birches, Django?"

"That is the name of the biggest camp of all: Auschwitz-Birkenau."

It had nothing to do with trees at all. All the trees had been cut down to make way for the humans that would be cut down.

"I can't believe Otto is going there," Blanca said softly. "He's so little. All he wanted was his mother."

"We can't be sure," Lilo said, but realized that her own words sounded empty to her.

No one was in the latrines when she walked in. Tears slipped down her cheeks. "He only wanted his mother. Just his mother," she whispered, then thought how Otto was right. They were living in a waking nightmare. Lilo slipped her hand into her pocket and touched the three chocolates, none of which she had unwrapped. There was the one from the first day of shooting. Then the one Tante Leni had given them when she had explained the scenes, and then the "bonus" one she gave each "urchin" for being such "wonderful, marvelous little actresses" as they mooned over her when she was dressing for her performance. She took them from her pocket and threw them down the hole of the latrine.

. . .

"Tell it again," Django asked.

He, Lilo, Rosa, Unku, and Blanca were up in the hay-loft, talking softly.

"I was coming back from the latrines by way of the water barrels," Lilo whispered. "The guards had gathered there to have a smoke and talk. There is a perfect place to hide to hear them. The bad guard —"

"That's Gunther," Django interrupted. Lilo sensed that he was just slightly jealous of the information she had discovered. Django liked to think of himself as the only one who could ferret out such vital intelligence, as he called it. Lilo had once referred to him as a "gatherer," which he deeply resented. "I don't gather. It sounds like I'm picking flowers in a garden. I run information. I am a runner."

Lilo continued: "Not ten minutes ago, I came across some astounding intelligence and I shall repeat it exactly as I heard it. The shooting will shut down here by the middle of the month and then the entire production will be moved to Babelsberg."

"Babelsberg?" Rosa, Unku, and Blanca said.

"Yeah, I have no idea where that is," Lilo replied

"Ha!" Django said. "I know exactly where it is." He looked quite pleased with himself. He could now resume his position as chief know-it-all.

"Where?" Blanca asked.

"Berlin."

"Berlin!" the three girls gasped. Berlin was the most important city, the most sophisticated city, in all of Europe.

"But is Babelsberg a city, too?" Lilo asked. As soon as the words were out, she regretted them. The question made her sound ridiculously ignorant.

"No," Django replied. "Babelsberg is simply the most important film studio in all of Europe. It is actually located just outside Berlin, in Potsdam. It makes sense, of course." Django was now speaking in his most authoritative voice. "You see, they have state-of-the art sound studios and can re-create scenes, especially the interior ones, all inside, protected from the weather." He paused dramatically. "Now, here's the problem." He held up a finger to command absolute attention. "We are not the only Gypsies available in Berlin. As you know, I am a veteran of the Marzahn camp, which is almost next door. They have a thousand Gypsies on tap there."

The girls groaned softly. "Wait!" Lilo said, her eyes brightening. "Look, we've only had a few weeks of shooting, but if they want to use us"—she held her hands out to indicate Rosa and Blanca—"for the street urchins, they can't just put in anybody. It will look funny in the film. I bet you anything that's where they sent Otto already—to Babelsberg."

Nobody met her eyes. Finally Django spoke: "You do

have a point. They'll need street urchins in Babelsberg. They haven't finished with all the town scenes yet, according to the script. They have to match the shots. I think it's called continuity. Same props, same extras. Did they do a lot of close-ups of you when you were peeking in the caravan, watching her get dressed?"

"Yes," the girls all answered. They were getting up to leave. Rosa yawned. "You know," she said, still yawning, "I had to keep reaching out, at least ten, twelve times, to touch the castanets she was going to dance with. They shot it from every which way."

When the other girls had left the hayloft, Lilo noticed that Django had suddenly grown quite still. "Django, are you becoming invisible?" she tried to joke.

"That's just the problem," he said.

"What do you mean?" she asked.

He slid his eyes toward Lilo. "Your mother is, too, Lilo, and me."

"What — too what?" she asked. A dark feeling was rising inside her.

"We — me and your mother — have been too invisible. We've been here, what? Almost three weeks. No close-up shots. Only long shots. We're replaceable. I mean, all they shot were my hands on that accordion. They could be anybody's hands."

"No! No!" She wanted to say, "No one could have

hands like yours." She loved his hands. She looked down and reached out, touching his right hand lightly.

"You mean replaceable with Marzahn Gypsies?"

Django nodded but said nothing.

Lilo returned to what she and her mother called their hay bale apartment. They had stacked nine bales of hay to make a small three-walled enclosure for their sleeping pallet. The fourth side of their sleeping area was the barn wall. The moonlight slid like a silver blade through the crack of the boards, casting its light on her mother's tired face. Lilo looked at it, not daring to stroke the cheek for fear of waking her. It was a wonderful face despite its gauntness. She was so thin that the outline of her teeth and gums made a slight impression on the space above her upper lip. Just the day before, she had lost one of her front teeth. It had simply dropped out. It was as if with not enough real food to chew, their teeth became loose — loose from disuse perhaps or most likely malnutrition. But at least her mother's bleeding had stopped.

Lilo simply had to figure out a way to get her mother to Babelsberg.

My mother is not replaceable. Nor is Django! Miteinander! She suddenly realized. The thought shocked her. There was indeed no one quite like Django. It was not just that he was so smart and that they all needed him to figure things out. It was that Django, despite all his annoying ways, had crept beneath Lilo's skin, inched his way into perhaps her heart, and now haunted the edges of her soul like a soft mist.

Lilo lay close to the barn board and pressed the side of her face against the crack. It was her new viewfinder through which she could scan the world for a place for herself, her mother, and Django. But all she could see now was the moon riding high and full in the crisp night air. *I must think about a close-up shot—no more long shots—for Django and Mama,* she told herself, then silently repeated, *No more long shots.* In her mind, she began framing their faces.

The moon was so perfectly round. Suspended in the night, it seemed to quiver slightly. But as Lilo watched the glinting orb through the crack in the wall, it did not slip away to another night in another world, but darkened and shrank. Then into her dreamless sleep, an eye floated up. "Call me Tante Leni." The voice giggled, and Lilo rolled over. Outside, the guards were roasting chestnuts in a grate. The mouthwatering scent drifted into the barn. She spied a shadow by the fence. At first she thought it was a small animal—a lamb perhaps, escaped from a lambing pen. But no! It was the little girl, crouching down where she had first met Lilo's mother. She looked around furtively, then ran off. What was she doing up this late, outside all by herself? Was she looking for Bluma?

Quietly Lilo got up. The barn door was no longer locked at night since they had enlarged the enclosure and built new latrines farther from the barn for the prisoners to have access to. It was only the fence prickled with barbed wire that was locked. There were rumors that they might electrify it, but so far they had not. Lilo slipped around to where the little girl had been standing. She saw that the dirt was loose around the fence stake. When she put her hand down, she felt heat. Scratching away the dirt, she nearly cried out when her fingers touched the chestnuts, still hot from the fire. She dropped them into the folds of her skirt and ran back to the barn.

Three minutes later, she had woken her mother, and they were peeling back the tough skin.

"Liesel!" her mother said, and her eyes twinkled. "What a little rascal."

"Is this the first time she has brought you things?"

"First time for food. But she is always bringing me little trinkets."

"Why didn't you tell me?" Lilo felt a prickle of jealousy.

"She made me promise not to, and I was really worried about her getting into trouble. But I did make a drawing of her kitten."

"Mama, that is dangerous. Really dangerous," Lilo said solemnly.

"But you don't understand. Her mama died last spring.

The girl is lonely. She worries that her father is going to marry the mean lady."

"What mean lady? There are several, I think," Lilo said, savoring the rich crumbs of the chestnut still on her tongue.

"Not Leni. Some rather wealthy lady in the next village over. And Liesel's older sister is in love with the head guard, Gunther."

Bluma reached out her hand and stroked her daughter's arm. Lilo felt foolish. But in truth she wanted her mother all for herself. *No more sharing,* she thought stubbornly. Sometimes it felt good to simply give in to her most infantile instincts if even for just a moment.

"Here, you take the last chestnut." Bluma pushed it toward her.

"Mama, I can't."

"Yes, you can," Bluma insisted.

"No, let's divide it." Lilo said.

"How do you divide a chestnut with no knife?"

"Peel it and use your teeth," Lilo replied.

"I don't have enough teeth. Remember?" She grinned, the dark hole making her smile ghoulish.

"Okay, I'll bite it." Lilo took the peeled nut, carefully bit it in two, and gave one half to her mother, vowing not to be jealous again.

Eleven

From the time she woke up the next morning, she was desperate to figure out a way to get her mother and Django into close-up shots. On this particular morning, the extras had to be taken to the set in a smaller bus in two loads, as the larger bus had broken down yet again. Django was in the first load, and by the time Lilo got to the enclosure, he was almost jumping up and down with excitement.

"You found a way for you and Mama to get in close-up shots."

"Not me, but definitely you and we'll think of something for your mother."

"I don't need a way. It's you and Mama who need a way."

"Don't quibble. This could really work out."

"But what about you?"

"I'm working on it. I'll organize something."

"All right. So what have you organized for me?"

"Tante Leni can't ride."

"Can't ride what?" Lilo asked blankly.

"A horse—*mein Gott!*" He slammed his palm into his head as if to say, how stupid can you be? "She almost fell off this morning."

"These old plugs? They hardly move," Lilo said, glancing over at the corral.

"But you can ride. They think it's too dangerous for Leni to try the riding scenes. But you . . . you can be her stand-in—or her ride-in! And they are going to shoot some riding scenes in Babelsberg indoors on the sound-stages." He laughed. "I already told them. Look, that fellow Harald is walking this way. He's going to ask you."

"But what about Mama? How do we get her in on this?"

Django sighed. "Do I have to think up everything? Make something up. An excuse for why you need her—I don't know." He sighed again. "Be inventive!" He looked around at the set. "Nothing's real here—the village is fake. The Spanish dancer is a Nazi. The shepherd is an Austrian ski instructor. It's all fiction. What's a little bit more?"

Django was right. Had Lilo not vowed to learn from Django so she could figure things out? Well, this was her first real test. The test was walking toward her—Harald

Reinl, the assistant director and choreographer. A thought suddenly came to her. Tante Leni's dancing wasn't very good. Whether it was because of his choreography or her lack of talent, Lilo wasn't sure. But she would have to pretend that Harald Reinl was the most fabulous choreographer. What else did she know about him? She certainly could see that Tante Leni kept him on a short leash. She had snapped at him that first day on the set—"*I don't give a goddamn what Arnold thinks. I fired him.*" *He doesn't want to get fired,* Lilo thought. He had also worried about Unku being too pretty. Lilo's mind was racing. She had to pull all these bits of information, scraps of things she knew about him, and work them into a piece so she and her mother could both go to Babelsberg.

"Where's the girl who can ride?" Harald Reinl asked.

Lilo raised her hand shyly. He strode up to her and put a hand under her chin to lift it. "What's your name?"

"Lilian Friwald."

"Well, Lilian, how would you like to ride a lovely horse in the movie? We'll pretend that you are Fräulein Riefenstahl. I know you were one of the street urchins in the close-up shots, but these will be mostly long shots. So I don't think it will matter. No one will know it's the same girl. You see, we need a shot of her riding on a horse through the entrance to the village, and then another when she rides out of the village with Pedro. Then some very distant shots of her riding against a setting sun with the mountains in the background. In those shots, we would like the horse to be cantering, but not a full gallop. What do you say?"

As if I have a say, Lilo thought.

She tucked her lips in and pressed them together as if she were thinking hard. "Hmm?" he said. She could tell that he was surprised that she had not answered more quickly. Lilo knew she had to play this right. "Where did you learn to ride?" he asked.

"My uncle Andreas, my mother's brother, was a trainer at the Spanish Riding School. We always went to the stud farm in Piber for our holidays."

"Ha!" He chuckled softly. "I thought Gypsies were always on holiday."

Ignore the insult, Lilo! Ignore it. He doesn't know any better.

"So you like this idea?" he pressed.

"Yes, I do. But my mother, may she always be present?" She looked up at him with a fragile half smile.

"Well, is she here?"

"Oh, yes, she plays one of the village peasants. You know, with the water jug on her head."

He looked over at the four or five women who were standing near the jugs they were soon to carry, then turned back to Lilo. "I don't understand. Why must she always be with you?"

"She knows horses." Lilo looked up and flashed him a different kind of smile, slightly embarrassed this time. "You know we're Gypsies. We're superstitious and . . ." She sighed. "Well, I have never fallen off when my mama was there. A horse has never shied when my mama was there."

"How close does she need to be?" His brow crinkled.

"Oh, just on the set. Near enough to see me and the horse."

"Well, I don't see any problem. We don't want you falling off the horse. That's settled. Go off to the costume lady to be fitted for your riding costume."

"What have you gotten me into, Lilo? I know nothing about horses."

"You're Uncle Andreas's sister. You have to know something. All those summers in Piber."

"But what am I supposed to say to a horse?"

"You don't have to say anything to the horse. Just stand there and look like you know horses. You know, pretend. It's the only way, Mama. Pretend! I needed you for the horse, not for myself," She paused. "For yourself, Mama." Then Lilo explained about Babelsberg. "Just look like you know horses."

Bluma touched her daughter's cheek. Lilo looked up into her face. Her mother was doing that funny thing with her mouth that meant she was trying not to cry, trying to look brave. "You and me, that's all we've got. Right? *Miteinander!*"

Miteinander—it was getting a bit more complicated because now . . . now, Lilo thought, there was Django. Where did he fit in? And for a moment, she was swept with guilt.

"Right?" her mother asked again.

"Right, Mama." She looked down and felt a horrible hollowness inside her. *What about Papa? Papa, where are you now?* She suddenly missed him terribly. Was he dead? If he was and yet she did not know it, he was still alive, in her mind. No one really died until you knew it. If she lost them both, she thought she might break, really break, break in two. For the first time, she wondered about his shop on Kirchestrasse. She pictured all the clocks waiting for him, all the watches, each in its cubby in the lined drawers, waiting . . . waiting . . . waiting. The gears frozen from neglect since no one was there to wind them. What would happen to them all?

Lilo was dressed for the scene in a riding skirt with a vest, and a kind of lady's sombrero, smaller than a man's. She caught a glimpse of herself in the wardrobe room and felt that she actually looked quite stylish. There were two horses waiting as she approached. When Lilo walked up, they were pasting some extra hair on one of the actor's head because he had a hairline that backed up halfway across his skull.

"Ach, now you know my beauty secrets." The man laughed. He turned around and put out his hand to shake Lilo's. She was stunned. This had never happened to her since she had been arrested. His hand was very soft and smooth, but he pressed her hand warmly in a truly friendly way. "Now, what is your name, dear?" He leaned forward a bit and looked into her eyes as he spoke.

"Lilian Friwald," she whispered.

"Mine's Bernhard Minetti."

Minetti looked no more like a Spaniard than Franz Eichberger did. His eyes were not as blue as Franz's — no eyes could be that blue — but were a misty gray with just a touch of blue. This was the man who was supposed to play the power-hungry, cruel Don Sebastian, but if anything, he reminded Lilo of one of her father's favorite clients for antique watches, Herr Haffner. He would never forget to bring a small gift for Lilo and often something for her mother whenever he came. Bluma declared that Herr Haffner was an old-fashioned Viennese gentleman and had the most exquisite manners of any man she had ever met. Lilo had trouble trying to fit the man standing before her with the cruel character he was being made to play. But as Django said, it was all fiction.

"And I understand that you are an excellent rider?"

"Yes, my mama's brother is"—she hesitated—"was a trainer at the Spanish Riding School in Piber." She detected a fleeting shadow cross the blue-gray mist of his eyes. "That is my mama, over there. She knows horses, too, but does not ride," she added quickly.

He looked up and walked over to her mother, who was in her black peasant costume.

"Frau Friwald." Frau! No one except Django had called her mother Frau in months. He was holding out his hand. "I am pleased to meet you, the mother of this excellent rider." Bluma was taken aback as well. But she nodded.

"Thank you, sir."

Leni then arrived with the head cameraman. "Albert, darling, show that painterly look of the darker grays of the landscape against the lighter ones of the sky. And then the two figures on horseback melt into the distance."

"Yeah, I'll have to use the long lens. Will the horses be walking, trotting, or what?"

"I think cantering."

Just then another man came running up. He was dressed identically to Bernhard Minetti. He gave Tante Leni a kiss, a bit more than the peck Lilo had seen Harald give her a few days before. Leni looked up at him with a glowing expression. Herr Minetti must have noticed Lilo staring at the two of them. He leaned forward and whispered to her, "Peter Jacob is my double for the cantering. But that's all." There was a trace of a smirk on Herr Minetti's face that gave Lilo a glimpse of the cruel side he would have to play.

Tante Leni told Lilo immediately that she was to address Peter Jacob as Lieutenant, as he was a lieutenant in the *Wehrmacht*. Lilo quickly surmised that like Franz, he had escaped going to war in order to be in the movie. As a double, he didn't quite match Minetti's height, Lilo observed, but then again, she herself was shorter than Leni.

Leni explained the scene to both Lilo and Peter. They were to come cantering over the top of a slight mound that was perhaps five hundred meters from where they were now standing. A marker had been placed at this point, and they were instructed to come to a halt. Then Leni and Minetti would climb on two wooden contraptions — they called them the rocking horses, but they were not child's toys. They were fake horses' heads with manes that matched the live horses and had been mounted with saddles on frameworks. The close-up would show the actors from their waists up with a bit of the horses' necks and the horns of the saddles in the frame.

Lilo and Lieutenant Jacob mounted their respective horses. She saw her mother making her way toward them. Bluma put out her hand, then nuzzled the horse's face and spoke some nonsense words in Sinti. *She's doing this per-fectly,* Lilo thought. *What an actress my mama is!* She turned away and smiled at Tante Leni and Albert, the camera-man, who were staring at her. "It always works," Bluma said, and flashed a smile. Lilo was stunned. Her mother was playing her part to the hilt.

After the scene had been shot, Lilo walked back to the "waiting pen," as the Gypsy extras had started to call it. As she and her mother drew closer, they heard the strains of a guitar. A real guitar playing live music. And it was a real Gypsy playing the music. Django! Lilo closed her eyes. She pictured his hands, long slender, yet callous from the work camps he had been in. Now with those same hands he was coaxing from that guitar wonderful rich, dark tones that colored the very air.

Django had organized a guitar. "Nothing to it," he said. "The actor who plays the guitarist wandered by the pen. I said to him, 'Let me have a look at that guitar.' He, of course, couldn't slide it through the wire mesh, but I said—just making this up, of course—I said, 'I know you don't really have to play it, but if you'd adjust the action . . .' He doesn't know what action is. So I explain that action is controlled by the height of the strings above the frets, and then I tell him to change the tension of the number two and the number three string. You see, I start throwing all these terms out there like crazy. He doesn't know what I'm talking about, but he's impressed. So just then an assistant cameraman comes by and Henrik— that's the actor's name—says, 'This guy knows what he's talking about. Can we bring him out of the pen?' Only he calls it the cage, which is sort of shocking, but it's the truth, ain't it? 'Can we bring him out of the cage and let him show me?' Well, the camera fellow is real interested. So I get out and begin to show them stuff. I am very particular to show them how the fingering can be done to look more realistic, and then I just start playing—not one of those stupid songs they had her dancing to but a real Gypsy song. But now the actor says, 'If we change the music, we'll have to change the dance.' And the cameraman says they are reshooting a lot of the tavern scenes in Babelsberg anyway."

Lilo gasped. "Django, you are amazing! If I'm a 'ride-in,' you're a what? A 'hands-in'?" They both laughed.

"Actually, I think the real name for what we are is 'double.' We're doubles."

The word struck Lilo oddly. *If only,* she thought, *there could be a double for our real lives as prisoners, and then we could leave that life behind and escape forever.*

Twelve

That little trailer," Janna said. She was a woman the same age as Lilo's mother.

"You mean the caravan?" Lilo asked.

"No, no, the fancy metal one that Fräulein Riefenstahl uses for her dressing room. I saw him go in there on my way to makeup. Then I heard thumps—bump, bump—then . . . 'Aaahh! Aaah!'"

Everyone broke out laughing.

"Shush, Janna, shush! They'll hear you," warned Ulrike, another water-jug lady.

"Not through my chattering teeth, they won't," Janna answered.

Lilo and a half dozen others were in the women's latrine back at the farm. The weather had turned chilly in the last few days, and although they had been provided with extra blankets, it was a challenge to sit long with one's panties down on a rough board with a hole over a trench. But the latrine was the best place for gossip. There were no walls between the toilets, and after being in so many camps, the lack of privacy did not faze them in the least. Despite the cold, all of them lingered to hear Janna's tale of Tante Leni and her lover, Peter Jacob, and their trysts in Leni's dressing room. Django was not the only source for information, especially of this nature. Janna and Ulrike actually had a competition going.

All the women were wrapped in thick horse blankets that had been left for them, but in addition they now wore thick socks. Liesel had left two pairs for Bluma, but Bluma had told her that she could not stand to wear the socks when others had none. The little girl had nodded solemnly, and then two days later, she left six pairs, the following day another eight, and then finally another ten. More than enough, since now there were only twenty-one prisoners.

Their teeth chattered as they gossiped away. Had gossip become a new kind of nourishment for them? Lilo looked down the line where they sat on the rough board over the smelly trench. Was this to be their life — the high point of their lives — sitting giggling in a latrine locked behind barbed wire? What did it matter if it was Krün or Babelsberg? And what would happen when the filming was finished? Surely then they would be sent east. Until now Lilo had thought only about surviving, day-to-day. But now she understood that she had to think about something else, beyond day-to-day survival—escaping before it was too late. Would her mother be strong enough? Might there be any chance to escape either on the way to Babelsberg or after they got there? Babelsberg was near Berlin. Berlin was a huge city. Could they disappear among the millions? And what about Django? Would he come? As Lilo thought of escape, the gossip went on.

"Mina's baby girl has a bad cough," Griselda, a toothless old woman, said. "She needs chest liniments and good steam."

"Fat chance of getting that."

"I bet they have hoof balm for their calves. That might work."

"What's the baby's name?" There was a silence, like a void in the night. No one had thought to inquire as to the baby's name. Had they never heard the mother call the little girl by name? Lilo could tell that they were all shocked. It was as if they had had to pare down their lives to only the sparsest detail. Anything else was a distraction.

"Well, you know," someone started to say, "the mother, Mina. She's very thoughtful. She always tries to sleep far from all of us so the child's crying won't disturb us."

"Yes," someone else said softly. It was as if they were suddenly aware that their own humanity was slowly slipping away.

Ulrike now spoke up, almost desperately, to change the subject: "What do you think of Fräulein Riefenstahl making eyes at Pedro—I mean Franz?"

Janna farted. Her timing was perfect. The tension was broken. They all roared at this.

"My sentiments exactly," said Irma, another water-jug lady.

"What's to stop her from having two?" Ulrike said. "My sources tell me that this woman has been with many men. The famous director Arnold Fanck—he was her lover."

"The one she fired," Lilo piped up. All eyes turned toward her. She was occupying the last seat in the row of the latrines.

"How do you know that?" Janna said, leaning forward to look at her at the end of the row. This kind of gossip was supposedly the province of the older women not young girls.

"My sources." Lilo winked, then got up from the board.

Perhaps it was ten minutes after Bluma and Lilo had returned from the latrines when they heard angry voices through the crack in the barn wall. "I'll be right back," Lilo whispered. She climbed to the hayloft to look out the window by Unku's sleeping pallet. It gave the best view down to where the voices were coming from.

"They're cold. This isn't about mollycoddling. The blankets aren't enough. They need heavier clothing."

Two long shadows sliced across the spray of moonlight on the ground below. It was Johan who spoke. "Look, just tell Fräulein Riefenstahl that she will not have any extras for her precious film unless she keeps them warm. They'll all come down with pneumonia. We hardly feed them as it is."

"I don't like your tone," Gunther replied.

"I don't like how you're screwing the farmer's oldest daughter."

A silence opened up between them as wide as the night. Unku and Lilo looked at each other, their eyes round with shock. "Oh, *sheka!*" Unku whispered the word for "shit."

Barely a quarter of an hour later, the two guards arrived, pushing wheelbarrows loaded with more blankets, as well as shawls and sweaters. Shortly after that, the large door of the barn slid open. The farmer's two daughters appeared. Each carried a pail with steam coming from it. Lilo saw the little girl scan the barn and knew immediately that she was looking for Bluma.

"Bring your bowls, please," Johan said as he stepped out of the shadows. "We want to give you something warm, and more is coming." The big sister leaned over to her little sister and whispered. She set her pail down and then ran toward the farmhouse. In a few minutes, the little girl returned with two more buckets.

It was a feast! Two pails of warm milk, two buckets of dumplings with boiled chicken. And still more was coming! Lilo ran to wake her mother. It was important for her to come, not just to eat but also to see the little girl and for the little girl to see her.

As soon as Liesel saw Bluma Friwald's face, she broke into a smile and ran toward her. She dipped her hand into the pocket of her dirndl. "For you, *Frau*," she said softly, and handed Bluma something. It was a *Pfannkuchen*, a bun stuffed with jam. And still warm! Bluma slipped it into her pocket.

"Liesel!" Her older sister scolded her then jerked her.

Lilo reached forward and grabbed her mother's hand.

"Mama, you have to be careful. You saw the sister didn't like when you did that."

She began to study her mother carefully. She did seem a bit stronger. She might have even put on some weight. Was she strong enough to get out of here? They had chicken and dumplings tonight, but it could all end tomorrow. Was there any chance they could get out? Make it to safety. But what was safe? Where was safety? The tiny cough of the nameless baby scratched the night. Lilo almost resented it. It was a distraction. She had to think, think hard. She was scared, scared of that older sister. She had to think about the possibilities of escape. But then the baby coughed again. Poor thing! She promised herself that tomorrow she would ask Mina her baby's name.

The very next day when Lilo got on the bus, she went up to Mina.

"I've been meaning to ask you your baby's name."

A fragile smile began to illuminate her face. "Brynna," she said softly.

"And is her cough better?"

"Oh, yes! Yes! Much better."

"Can I have a peek at her?" Lilo asked, since the infant was bundled up.

"Oh, she's sleeping now. So peacefully, I hate to disturb her."

"Oh, sure. I understand. But I am so happy that Brynna is feeling better."

"Thank you," Mina said. Her eyes suddenly seemed shiny with tears. Lilo couldn't help but feel better. Little effort had brought so much pleasure to Mina.

As soon as they got to the set, it was announced that the following day they would be leaving for Babelsberg.

The numbers of those scheduled for transport to Babelsberg were posted in the cage.

When they disembarked, there was a great rush toward the cage.

"You're in! You're in, both of you! And me, too!" Django said, turning to Lilo and her mother. Bluma flung her arms around Lilo.

"*Miteinander!*" her mother sobbed in her ear.

Rosa, Unku, and Blanca were also in. In fact most of the prisoners except a few very old ones who rarely came to the set were on the list.

"Are you in?" Lilo said, making her way over to where Mina stood.

"Yes, yes! And so is Brynna. She'll get to see the big city."

"All this roaring hasn't woken her up?"

"No, she's still sleeping, thank God. Now that the cough is gone, she breathes easier."

Thirteen

They had left in a caravan. Fourteen vehicles in all. One for the Gypsies, several large trucks for the camera equipment, sets, and costumes, and an open-sided ventilated truck for the horses. Tante Leni rode in a special black sedan with the assistant director, Harald Reinl, and Franz Eichberger.

Lilo sat next to her mother, watching the landscape unfold. It reawakened her dreams of escape. She didn't want to tell her mother until she was sure her mother was strong enough and she had a plan. They were told that the trip to Babelsberg would take one night and two days. The extras were to sleep in the bus, while the crew and Leni would be put up at a hotel in the town where they planned to stop. No one, of course, had told them which town that would be. There would be stops so they could relieve themselves, but armed guards would accompany them for these necessities. In fact, the number of armed guards had been tripled for the journey.

They had been under way perhaps for three hours when Lilo got the faintest whiff of a disturbing odor. It seemed to be coming from behind her. Had someone had an accident? She dared not turn around. Within a few minutes, though, she sensed that other people were noticing. An *Aufseher* from the front of the bus began to walk down the aisle. He was met by another coming from the rear. They conferred for a few seconds. Then they continued to walk in opposite directions, their nostrils twitching.

Then *"Mein Gott im Himmel!"* one of them roared. *"Es ist ein Kind—ein totes Baby."*

"A dead baby!" Lilo gasped.

"Nein, nein." It was a woman's voice.

The bus slowed down abruptly and pulled to the side of the road. A furor had broken out in the back of the bus. The *Aufseher* came racing forward. He was carrying something. Bluma, who was on the aisle, screamed.

"Mama, what is it?"

"The baby. Mina's baby."

A gun went off in the bus.

"Achtung! Everyone be quiet. Sit down or be shot."

"Oh, my God," Lilo whispered. She was looking out the window. The guard who had raced from the back of the bus was by the side of the road. He wound up his arm in a pitching motion and released. The bundle sailed into the sky, the flawlessly blue sky on this cold winter day. There was another shriek as Mina raced off the bus. *Run, run as fast as you can . . . You'll never . . .* The crack of several guns, machine guns, rived the air. Everyone was pressed to the windows of the bus. They saw the spasmodic jerks of Mina's body, which for three seconds looked as if it were dancing as the bullets tore into her. Blood splattered everywhere, and then it was over. The body crumpled on the ground. A stunned silence fell upon the bus.

From the window, Lilo observed some of the other guards and now Leni and Harald striding up the roadside. Leni wore a stylish hat and her fancy alligator boots.

"Don't look at her," Bluma rasped. But Lilo could not tear her eyes away from Leni. She was arguing with someone — a guard.

"Are you crazy, Lieutenant?" Leni shrieked. "We don't have time for such nonsense. I suppose you want to fetch a priest for this burial as well. My allegiance is to the Führer. We have to be in Babelsberg by tomorrow. This film is going over budget already. I shall hold you personally responsible. It is the Third Reich that is financing this. Do you want to explain how we took an extra day here?" The lieutenant was trying to say something, but Lilo couldn't hear it.

"What do you mean it won't take a day? I don't care if it takes a minute. Now, be reasonable, sir. Look." Leni swept her hand dramatically toward the sky. "Nature is taking care of this already."

Lilo looked to where Leni was pointing. Three buzzards were carving arcs in the porcelain-blue sky. "God takes care of these things. God is efficient, and so am I!"

She strode away. Several guards came up and kicked Mina's body into the drainage ditch.

But so far . . . so far from her baby, Lilo thought, for the baby had been flung into the field. *Miteinander.*

Lilo and her mother folded themselves into each other's arms. Bluma stroked Lilo's head. How long had the baby been dead? Was she dead when Lilo had asked to see her on the bus? That was yesterday morning, more than twenty-four hours ago. Had she died in the night? *Poor Mina. Poor Brynna.*

BABELSBERG

Winter 1940–1941

Fourteen

Quiet on the set! Bring up the wind. Action!" Lilo dug her heels into the flanks of Chico, the horse she had ridden through the archway of the make-believe village of Roccabruna. Everything, though not everyone, had been transported to the Babelsberg studios—horses, the tavern, the scenery flats of the buildings of Roccabruna. If the village of Roccabruna was a fiction, Babelsberg Studios were a fiction upon a fiction. The studio buildings stretched over hundreds of acres. There was not just one counterfeit village but entire cities and mountain ranges that had been created, facades designed and built by the scenery department. Bring up the wind! Bring up the sun! Bring up New York! Paris! *Bring up anything*, Lilo thought, *except the real world.*

"Cut!" screamed Leni. Now those small eyes blazed as she walked toward Peter Jacob and Lilo on their horses.

God, Lilo prayed, *what have I done wrong?* The scene that Lilo had witnessed by the side of the road when Leni had screeched at the guard had convinced Lilo that this woman was completely crazed, perhaps not even human. Somehow the murder had paled next to Leni's reaction to the guard who had apparently wanted at least the semblance of a decent burial for the woman. But *reaction* seemed like a slight word. It suggested some sort of human response when there was absolutely nothing human about her behavior. Lilo wondered what might have triggered it, for there seemed to be a continuing deterioration of her behavior with frequent outbursts on the set.

"Peter!" Leni hissed. "You can't ride a horse when you're hungover! And it's not just liquor I smell on you"— her voice dropped—"but whores!" The color had drained from her face. The makeup lay eerily on her skin like fresh paint. "You keep to stage left so your shadow falls on the Gypsy girl, understand!"

"Yes, Leni!" She shot him a poisonous look. "I mean, yes, Fräulein Riefenstahl."

"You don't know what you mean!" she muttered, and stomped away.

On the fifth take, they got it right.

• • •

Life was better in Babelsberg if only because it was warmer. They were kept not in a barn but in an empty soundstage. It was warm, and there were toilets, not latrines, and even two showers. Lilo felt incredibly lucky that the invention of her mother as her good-luck charm had worked so far. She found it amusing how her mother had so completely gotten into the part. Lilo teased her that if this war was ever over, she and Bluma would be riding side by side in Piber on the Lipizzaners. Extras and crew alike seemed more relaxed at Babelsberg. It was more of a community than the farm. It was a real village in the sense of film production. There were entire buildings devoted to stage carpentry. There were kitchens that provided food for the cast and crews of each film under production on a soundstage.

Since they were not as confined as they had been in Krün, the doors with the locks were mostly to keep people out—thieves, of course, for there was so much expensive equipment, but also starry-eyed autograph seekers. The film slaves were always indoors on the soundstage. There was little danger of any of them wandering off, unlike when they were in the countryside. Outside, winter had set in. It was warm inside, and they had hot food. These conditions were as effective as the locks on the doors. Lilo's thoughts of escape began to dwindle.

Twenty additional Gypsies had been imported from

the nearby Marzahn camp as extras. Django was pleased to see an old friend of his, a boy named Erich who was a bit younger and half the size of Django, whom one could not exactly call big.

The years Erich had spent in Marzahn since Django had last seen him had shrunk him from the size of a proper fifteen-year-old to that of a nine- or ten-year-old. Django was determined to fatten him up. It was a lot easier organizing food in Babelsberg, and Django had figured out who might be sympathetic in the kitchens. Bribery, it would seem, was out of the question, as what did any film slave own? What currency did they have to trade? However, Django devised a fictional currency to match the fictional world they lived in. The Gypsies' roles as extras put them in very close contact with the stars—Bernhard Minetti; Franz, whom there was already buzz about in the nightlife of swanky Berlin cabarets; and Maria Koppehoeffer, who played the wealthy woman the marquis was supposed to marry but did not love.

The men and women who worked in the kitchens and the custodial staff of the buildings rarely got very close to these stars, but they longed for the smallest memento of a star. Any number of discarded handkerchiefs and an occasional autographed picture made their way to the staff. However, the best negotiation that Django ever made was to slip a screenplay written by a kitchen worker into Arnold Fanck's briefcase. It was one of those rare occasions when the renowned director, who had been fired by Leni, visited the set. Arnold Fanck was one of the most important directors not just in Germany but in all of Europe. His visits to the set had been seldom and only in the company of the chief executive of the studio when certain high-level Nazi Party officials were escorted in for behind-the-scenes glimpses of moviemaking. But on one visit Django had pulled it off with the screenplay. "No guarantee he will love it, but it is in his briefcase. He can't help but see it." The kitchen worker and aspiring screenplay writer Dieter was eternally grateful. So this single act more or less opened the kitchen to Django and the rest of the film slaves.

Today Lilo and the other urchins were standing around in a small area near the village fountain. They were filming a market day scene, and an assistant to the assistant to the assistant director was marking the places where they were to stand. Franz was not in this scene at all, but nevertheless, he was hanging around near a vegetable cart that was being set up with onions and potatoes. Some potatoes spilled and rolled toward the urchin girls. Franz raced over to help the prop fellow collect them. As Franz was on his knees collecting the vegetables, he lingered by the hem of Unku's skirt. Lilo watched as he gave the skirt a light tug. A radiance broke across Unku's face, obliterating the grime.

Until that moment, Lilo had sometimes been tempted to believe that her suspicions were merely figments of her imagination. Perhaps it was wishful thinking. But now she knew they were not imaginary. *This is bad. No, worse than bad — dangerous.* She suddenly recalled what she had long repressed — the dozens of other instances when Unku and Franz had somehow managed to be within yards, if not feet, of each other. For the rest of the day, a debate raged within Lilo as to whether or not she should say something to Unku.

Fifteen

What is she doing?" Lilo whispered to Rosa and Django while they were standing at the edge of the set. Fifty feet from them, Leni was huddled with Franz. She had snaked her arm around his waist in a very intimate way. She was giggling and pressing her cheek to his shoulder.

"Flirting," Rosa said. "What else would you call that?"

"Tante Leni," Django sighed. It was the sigh of an old man. "This is not simple flirting."

"What else is it?" Lilo asked.

"I have it on good authority that Fräulein Riefenstahl had a huge fight with Herr Jacob over his philandering. She wants to make him jealous." Lilo tried to look discreetly at Django. Could he possibly know what she knew about Unku and Franz? If he did, he would have said something.

Django, the ultimate insider, loved his "intelligence." It would be a blow to him that Lilo knew something he didn't, but she was fairly sure that his "good authority" had not informed him of this twist in the romantic entanglements of Fräulein Riefenstahl.

Her dread started to build. She felt that she must tell Unku that she knew what was going on between her and Franz. She turned to find her and saw that she was not five feet away. Bluma and Blanca were talking to her, but Unku's eyes were locked on Franz and Leni, huddled at the edge of the set. Her face had been transformed into a mask of disbelief and beneath it hatred. Raw hatred. *Don't be stupid,* Lilo wanted to say. *You are not the one who is supposed to be jealous. Peter Jacob is. Not you!*

Five minutes later, Lilo witnessed another accidental brushing up between Unku and Franz. A word was exchanged. *Don't touch her,* Lilo prayed. *For God's sake, don't touch her.* He walked about ten paces away and then turned and looked back at her. The yearning in his eyes was so intense, Lilo felt as though she should look away. Was she the only one who could see this? No! Not the only one! Harald Reinl was staring at Unku. He saw it all. *He knows,* Lilo thought. *He knows!*

She vowed to confront Unku that same day before the shooting finished. But when she did speak to her, she wanted to have all her "jewels in order," as her father would say before beginning a watch repair. She suddenly felt crushed by the memory of her father bending over the watches with his tweezers, delicately inserting the tiny jewels between the rotating steel parts. The jewels, which were the bearings, had to be perfectly placed for the movements of the watch. There was an orderliness to the way her father worked. *Where is he now?* she wondered. *Is he alive or dead?* Had he been fed into the death machine? *Devoured?* She shut her eyes. Could Django find out anything? If he could slip a script into Arnold Fanck's briefcase, could he make a connection with someone who might know something about her father? Her head ached. It was as if her brain were being crushed between the two movable jaws of a mammoth vise—her desperate longing for her father and this dangerous game that Unku, her dear friend, was playing. Could she even hope to get her jewels in order to find out about her father and help Unku? At the moment, it seemed more realistic to help Unku avert an impending disaster.

She decided to go to Django with both problems. When she found him, he was practicing the fingering of the next musical number with Henrik the guitarist.

"I have to talk to you now!"

"Now? Can't you see I'm busy here with Henrik?

Henrik is doing so well. He's going to be able to play better than me soon."

"Go on, Django." Henrik laughed and gave him a pat. "Go talk to your pretty girlfriend."

"I'm not his girlfriend," she shot back. She immediately regretted it, for she caught just the shadow of a look she had never seen cross Django's face. She was not sure what to call it—crestfallen? But the face had not fallen. It was rather like the moment just before a house of cards begins to slip. Did he think he was her boyfriend, or was he just her friend? Their friendship had been short but ran deep. What exactly was he? she wondered. She reached out and took his hand and gave it a gentle squeeze.

"All right," he said quietly.

They walked off just a few feet. "Can Harald Reinl be trusted?"

He looked at Lilo with a touch of scorn. "No. Why?"

"I'll tell you soon, but tell me why he can't be trusted."

"Because he is insecure."

"Why is he insecure?"

"Because he's not Arnold Fanck. Doesn't have half the talent, not one-tenth."

"And he wants Leni to like him?"

"Adore him, but not as a lover. He's like everyone else around here. He wants to be a star—direct a film of his own — really his own. Leni is his ticket to fame. He'd do anything for her."

"I was afraid so," Lilo replied, and looked down at her bare feet. They were caked with fake mud.

"What is it, Lilo?" He reached out with his hand lightly and touched her elbow. "You can tell me."

I owe this to him, she thought. But *owe* was the wrong word. Django and she didn't trade. They didn't barter or bribe. She could not reduce this to anything so common.

"What is it, Lilo?" he repeated. "There's something more troubling you."

"There are two things, really."

"All right, two things. What are they?"

"Look, Django, you have so many connections with the Marzahn prisoners. Is there any chance that any of them have connections with ones who were at Buchenwald, anyone at all who would know about my father?"

"That's a hard one. I can try and check, but I doubt it. What is the second thing?"

"It's Unku — her and Franz."

"No!" It was more of an exhalation, a breath, than a word. If Lilo had thought this "intelligence" would be a bruise to his self-esteem, she was wrong.

"This is bad, Lilo. Really bad."

"I know."

"What are you going to do?" he asked.

Me? she thought. *He's asking me?* It was an odd reversal. She took a deep breath and began to speak.

"I'm going to find her right now and talk to her. Tell her I know. Tell her it has to stop."

"You can't tell her right now. There are too many people around. Look who's coming over."

It was Tante Leni.

"All right, my little urchins, gather round!" She waggled her fingers, summoning them toward her. "Now this is the market scene, where I shall come wandering through and you children must tag after me again like you did when we were in Krün and I first arrived in the village of Roccabruna in my caravan wagon." She paused and looked about. "Why's that one not coming, Harald?"

"Who, dear?"

"The urchin over there. Get her."

It was Unku. *Good God!* Lilo thought. *This is already spinning out of control.* Why didn't Unku come when they were summoned?

When she arrived, it got worse. Unku was no actress. A scowl was engraved on her face. *Stop it, stupid girl! Stop it!*

"You always take your time like this, Miss? When I say 'come,' you come!" Leni snapped. One would think that Unku would look down contritely, sheepishly, but no. She looked straight into those beady eyes, her own amber eyes blazing like licks of fire. Observing this scene, one might have imagined that Leni Riefenstahl had met her match in this game, Lilo thought. But of course the dice were loaded.

"But I love him!" Unku whispered hoarsely hours later. Lilo stared at the two glistening tracks of tears that ran down Unku's cheeks. She stared so hard, they seemed like twin rivers. She felt herself slipping into them, dissolving into the streams. She began to stammer.

"I—I—I know. I know. But it is dangerous. *She* is dangerous. She is very close to Hitler. To all the big Nazis."

"What does Hitler care about some Roma girl's love affair with an actor?"

Lilo struggled to find the words. "It's not that. Hitler doesn't care. But Leni gets what she wants. She went to great pains to make sure you looked as ugly as possible. She made the hairdresser chop off your hair. And she shaved that bald spot."

Unku's eyes twinkled. "Franz loves it. He kisses it." She touched it with two fingers. She wrinkled her nose. "I hope she keeps shaving it!" Pure defiance! Lilo was getting nowhere. She knew it, so Lilo let her curiosity get the best of her. "So where, or when, does he get a chance to kiss it?

Where do you go?" Unku tossed her head back and laughed even though the tears were still wet on her cheeks.

"Oh, Lilo, you can bribe anyone here."

"You bribed a guard?"

"Not me. Franz."

"But when? I always see you."

"Do you stay awake all night?"

"No, but . . ."

"I get up around two or three in the morning. I go to the toilets."

"You meet him in the toilets?"

"No! Don't be ridiculous. At the end of the hall, where the toilets are, there is a door. It's locked, but Franz arranges for the guard to unlock it at a certain time."

"And then where do you go? I hope it's more romantic than the toilets."

"Not much." She laughed. "We go to a service area. It's an electrical room. Has a high-voltage sign on the door."

"God, I hope you don't get electrocuted."

"No, don't be silly. It's the perfect place. There is the deep humming of all these machines that drive the power of the whole building. It's perfect."

"Perfect? Doesn't sound very romantic to me."

Unku's shoulders slumped. "Lilo, have you never made love?" Lilo felt the blood rush to her face. "No, of course not. You've never had a boyfriend." But Unku did not say this in a patronizing way. She patted Lilo's hand gently. "You'll see."

An unsettling thought struck Lilo at that moment. *I could very easily die a virgin.* She immediately felt guilty even having such a thought, for on the scale of horrors she had seen in the past several months, beginning with her family's arrest, then her mother's sterilization, and finally the murder of Mina, she knew that dying a virgin was rather minor. But still she thought it wasn't fair. She was suddenly furious. She knew that she was like a child crying out "No fair!" in a game. She might be forever childish. She might die before she even reached sixteen. She might die a child and a virgin.

Unku lowered her voice and continued. "When you make love, you sometimes make a little noise, and the thrum of the machinery —"

Now she was being patronizing, Lilo thought, and held up her hand. "Don't! You don't need to explain. I get the picture." She took a deep breath. "Look, the point is that this is dangerous. You're playing with fire, with this Franz."

"Don't call him 'this Franz.'" Unku said this almost mournfully. Lilo instantly regretted her words. To call him "this Franz" was harsh. She knew it. For Unku, he was Franz Eichberger and not merely "this Franz." She loved him. The sadness in Unku's eyes was almost unbearable.

What right did she have telling her not to do this? Unku was putting only herself in danger. Not Lilo. Not anyone else. And so if she was risking all for love in a world where hatred ruled, wasn't this a good thing? A hopeful thing?

Sixteen

Every day Lilo was hearing people on the set placing bets on when the action would start on the eastern front. Some said by March, but March was coming soon, just a month away. They had been in Babelsberg now for over three months. The filming continued, seemingly impervious to the war.

The set painters had worked all night on the fake sunset that the doubles, Lilo and Peter Jacob, were to be riding against. It looked all too garish to Lilo, but then the film was black-and-white so what did it matter? The lighting for this scene was tricky, however, as the two of them on their horses would be shot in silhouette against the sky. A row of arc lights had been dropped from the ceiling to create the harsh lighting required for the scene.

A thick cushion was put into the saddle for Lilo so she would appear taller, at least three inches taller, to match Leni's height. The silhouette shot would emphasize any contrasts in stature more than the usual distance shots of them riding. Peter Jacob, aside from being an excellent rider, was the exact same height as Franz and one-half inch taller than Minetti—the ideal double for the horseback-riding scenes. But right now as he strode toward his mount, he had a deep scowl engraved on his face.

"Bitch!" Peter Jacob muttered as he swung his leg over and settled in the saddle. Lilo heard him. He might not have thought so, but she did. He might not care if she heard him or not. But then Lilo realized that actually he would like to engage her in conversation. He gestured with the reins in his left hand toward "the scene" going on beyond camera range.

Leni had plopped herself in Franz's lap and was stroking his cheek. She was a great actress, Franz less so, but he was trying. Most likely he was afraid of losing his job and being sent back to the front—the eastern front. Skiing to Russia, Django would say. Then it was as if Peter Jacob were reading her mind. He slid his eyes toward her. "Not much of an actor, is he?" He laughed. "Perhaps we should do a bit of a counterattack." He leaned toward Lilo as if to kiss her. *Holy Mother!* Then in the same moment, there was a sizzling sound, followed by a loud crack of one of the arc lights as it shorted. Sparks flew. Both horses reared up. Lilo saw the ground coming toward her. Horses crashed. Hooves struck the air. *My mother!*

"Stop the horses!" someone shouted.

"Get the Gypsy woman."

Oh, my God, Lilo was thinking. *They think Mama really does know horses!* But then a worse thought: *I am not supposed to fall off when Mama is here. What will they do?*

But Lilo was flat on the ground. Bluma and Django were both on their knees, hanging over her. "Are you all right?" It was Django speaking. She realized then that her head was in his lap. He was stroking her hair with those lovely long fingers. Bluma Friwald appeared absolutely frozen with fear.

"I'm fine," Lilo said. She bent one leg and brought her foot to rest flatly on the floor, then the other foot. Nothing seemed broken. Her shoulder hurt a bit. The stupid hat she wore as part of the costume had a very stiff crown, and it had somehow slipped back, which had helped protect her head when she hit the ground. The horses appeared to have been caught and were being led back to where the scene began.

Leni meanwhile was trying to cradle Peter Jacob in her arms.

"Get away, you ugly bitch!" He staggered to his feet and began walking away.

"Where are you going?" she cried.

A hush fell on the set. The only sound was that of the horses breathing. Lilo turned her head toward Peter Jacob. Then every head on the set turned. "To see Eva, my darling Eva. Half your age, you crone." He spat out each word and continued walking.

Leni suddenly seemed to shrink. She looked old and frail, even insignificant, until Lilo saw her eyes. A deep shudder coursed through her. She knew that worse was still to come. *So dangerous . . . so dangerous*—that was all she could think.

When Lilo returned the next day to reshoot the scene, the first thing she saw was Leni getting up from Franz's lap. She got up and walked toward her. Lilo felt as if she were caught in the beam of those closely set eyes. "We have a wonderful new double, and I have already given him his instructions. But we've altered it a bit. Instead of you being on the left side of the double, as you were with Peter, you can ride just a bit in front."

Lilo nodded. "Yes, yes. I'll tell my mother to go to stage left, then."

"Is that really necessary? It didn't seem she was of much use yesterday. You fell off." She gave a toss of her head as she said this and laughed lightly. Was that a threat? Lilo wondered. But despite her laugh, despite the coy toss of her head, Lilo felt the heat of Leni's anger—not at her in particular, just the general devouring anger of a woman who had been scorned. Over her shoulder, Lilo saw Franz get up and shake his head ever so slightly as if in disbelief. *She is a monster,* Lilo was thinking, and people were her playthings as she turned love to rage. But Lilo wondered what Franz would turn his love to, his love for Unku. Indifference?

"Please let my mother stand by." She raised one finely plucked eyebrow. "Tante Leni," Lilo added quickly.

Her face broke into a smile. "Oh, silly girl. If you want your mama, sure!"

Why was she not relieved? Lilo wondered. But she was not.

"This woman is crazy," Bluma murmured to Lilo late that night. Neither of them was asleep. It was not simply worrying about her mother or Unku that kept Lilo awake. Her shoulder still hurt from the fall. She was bruised all the way down one side of her body.

"You just noticed?" Lilo said.

"I don't understand what she's doing with Pedro What's-His-Name."

"Franz—Franz Eichberger. She was trying to make Peter Jacob jealous."

"But he isn't around now. So how can he see them?"

"I don't know, Mama. Maybe she takes Franz out to nightclubs or something, goes dancing with him and hopes to run into Jacob. I don't know. Go to sleep."

Bluma sighed and turned over. But she was not going to sleep. Lilo knew it. Three or four minutes later, her mother whispered, "You think Papa is still alive?"

Lilo wanted to say, *Of course he is.* She wanted to say, *Papa is tough.* But she knew her father had a heart condition. He was not that tough. He could so easily be dead.

"You heard about Mauthausen?" her mother asked.

"What?"

"From that woman you know."

"You mean one of the water-carrying women?"

"Yeah, she was in the scene yesterday. She's a nice lady for—" Her mother, Lilo knew, was about to say *for a Roma,* but she caught herself. "Anyhow, she says at that camp Mauthausen, there is this 'staircase of death,' they call it. It goes down into a stone quarry, and the prisoners are forced to carry stones up from the bottom of the quarry. She says there is a saying that each rock costs the life of a man. She heard that her husband and son both died there."

"Don't listen to her, Mama. She doesn't know anything."

But that probably wasn't true. The Marzahn prisoners

seemed to know things that others did not. Perhaps it was because they had been in a camp so close to Berlin. Also a lot of other prisoners had come through Marzahn on their way to other camps. There was a grapevine of information. This was what Lilo had been counting on when she had asked Django to try to find out news of her father. However, with the arrival of the Marzahn prisoners came more rumors of Poland and what was going on in the camps there, especially Auschwitz. There was talk of a giant death machine being readied into which prisoners would be fed. A word began to circulate: *porajmos.* It meant "devouring" in many dialects of the Romani language.

Bluma yawned and said sleepily. "Maybe you're right." Lilo knew her mother was lying. *And,* thought Lilo, *Mama knows that I know she is lying. She knows that I am lying when I tell her that the Marzahn woman knows nothing. More fiction. And yet she falls asleep. And so will I.*

And yet she did not fall asleep. She began thinking about Django. Her feelings were changing subtly, she could tell. She had known this ever since her first conversation with Unku about Franz, when she had wondered if she might ever want the kind of intimacy Unku had described. The problem was not really dying a virgin at all. The problem was one of space. Did she have enough room in her heart to love someone beyond her parents during this horrible war? She must look after herself and her mother. To love someone else was a luxury she could not afford. It was dangerous.

It was in the small hours of the night when deep in her sleep Lilo heard a tiny crash. A shattering of glass. In her dream, she looked down. All around her on the concrete floor, pieces of a watch were scattered. There was the escapement wheel with its notches. All sorts of little screws — the bridge screw, an anchor screw, ratchet-wheel screw, wheels, winding pinions strewn about. Lilo knew that she had to assemble all these parts or else her father would die.

"I don't know how. I keep telling you I don't know how, Tante Leni."

"What good are you, darling? First you tell me that your mama knows horses, but look what happened, and now you tell me your father is a watch expert, buys and sells antique watches, repairs them. But this is a lie, too? You lie! You lie!" She turns to walk away. Lilo gasps. Leni is naked. There is no back to her dress. Her bare buttocks seem to twitch. Lilo is seized with a fit of giggles — giggles and fear. *I cannot laugh. She will kill me.* She slams her hand to her mouth.

Suddenly she was awake, awake and biting her own hand! And not laughing. Still, in this moment, she was fearful not for her mother, nor for her father, nor herself, but for Unku. She looked over. Unku's cot was empty.

Lilo inhaled sharply. Never had an empty cot seemed more alarming. She went to the toilets. Unku was not there. How could she dare to sneak out after what had been going on? Had she listened to nothing Lilo had said? It was four in the morning. She must be coming soon, Lilo thought. There was nothing she could do, so she returned to her own cot. But sleep was impossible. She decided to go back to the toilets and wait for Unku to come through that door marked with the high-voltage warning.

She finally fell asleep with her head against the base of the toilet. She slept deeply, and then hearing the door creak, she jerked awake, hitting her head.

Wrong door! She cursed silently. It was the woman from Mauthausen who had told Bluma about the staircase of death. She looked at Lilo oddly and then shrugged as if to say, *So what else is new? She sleeps with a toilet for a pillow.* But it was in that moment that Lilo knew deep in her gut that Unku was gone. Gone for good.

"She's gone," Lilo said in a low voice when she arrived on the set an hour later. Django looked up from the guitar he was tuning. Confusion swept across his face, and then his eyes, already dark, became absolutely black.

"Unku?"

She nodded.

Django did not say "Are you sure?" or "How do you know?" Instead he turned his head toward Franz, who sat in a chair, looking straight down toward the floor. It was a posture of total defeat.

"Do you think he knows where she has gone?" Lilo asked.

"Don't you dare ask him. Don't go near him." Django grabbed her elbow and dug in his fingers. "If she"—he nodded toward Leni's dressing room, where she was speaking to the wardrobe mistress—"in any way connects you with Unku or him, you're finished. Don't say a word— promise me." He then concluded with an old Romani pro- verb: "*Makh ci hurjal ande muj phanglo.*" A fly won't fly into a mouth that is shut. "In other words, keep it shut!"

He almost spat the words out. Lilo rolled her eyes, and Django reached out and touched her shoulder lightly. "Try not to worry too much. *So ci del o bers, del caso.*" It was another old saying: What a year may not bring an hour might. Tears sprang to her eyes. He put his arm around her and crunched her to his chest. "It's all right," he said soothingly. "I mean, I know it's not all right, but I can't stand to see you so sad. I think it could be all right. It might not be so bad as you think."

Django was trying to give her hope. Hope! She was so confused at this moment. Her feelings for Django welled up within her. Would he speak of hope to everyone as he did to her in this moment? If he had room in his heart to hope for her . . . She could not complete the thought. But was there really any reason she should hope for anything and last of all love? Should any of these film slaves hope? They were all abandoned, and yet it was virtually impossible to kill hope. Did she not look around twenty times every hour hoping to see Unku?

She waited for Tante Leni to appear. But so far she had not come. They were told that they would be reshooting some scenes from the previous week. While Lilo was in makeup having her feet made to look dirtier, a new extra was brought over. She could see immediately that the girl was tall. Tall like Unku. Tall and quite ugly and wearing the same rags Unku had worn. That put the seal on Unku's fate. Lilo knew that there was a term for such prisoners who simply vanished. *Nacht und Neblen*. Night and Fog. It was into this night and fog that prisoners simply dissolved—untraceable, never to be seen or heard from again. Their deaths never confirmed, these people were condemned to wander forever through this netherworld, this purgatory of nonexistence that was neither death nor life.

A chair toppled over backward, and out of the corner of her eye, Lilo saw Franz jump up and storm off the set. But people barely took notice. Bella, who was now smearing the sludge in Lilo's hair to make it look dirty and tangled, made only a tsking sound. "Stupid boy," she muttered. "He wants to go to the front, I believe. He should think of his poor mama."

So they all know! Lilo thought.

SARENTINO

Spring 1941

Seventeen

Mama, try not to worry. Hardly anyone is being taken to Sarentino."

"*Miteinander, miteinander,*" Bluma whimpered.

By the second week in May, shooting had completed in the Babelsberg studios. It was announced that they would all be returning to Krün and some, a very few, would continue on to Sarentino, a village in the Dolomites of Italy, for further shooting.

Lilo and Django were included but not the water-jug ladies or Rosa and Blanca. Bluma's reputation with the horses had never recovered from the disaster on the set that day. For the first time, she would be separated from her daughter. *Miteinander*—the word rang in both Lilo's and her mother's heads, tolling ominously like mourning chimes from a bell tower.

There were several men, however, who would be employed for the backbreaking labor of digging the lake for the Italian scenes. Django was being brought not to dig but to pluck the strings as a hand double for the guitar that Franz was supposed to be able to play.

"It will be okay, Frau Friwald," Django said with conviction. "I don't think we'll be gone that long." He and Lilo spent the entire bus trip back to Krün trying to console her.

"Look, Mama! Look who's here to greet you," Lilo whispered as they got off the bus at the farm. Liesel was there, waiting in front of the barn. Her face brightened as she caught sight of Bluma. "Mama, for her sake put on a smile."

Bluma looked at Lilo, a sad irony in her eyes as if to say "for her sake." In that moment, Lilo knew that her mother was entertaining the same thought she had had weeks before when she had wondered if she had enough room in her heart to care for anyone beyond her parents. Caring was a luxury ill afforded.

They had hoped to find Unku back at Krün. But there was not a trace of her. The extras who had been left there over the winter and not gone to Babelsberg had not seen her. Somehow these extras had survived the winter, mostly due to the kindness of Johan, the good guard. The other guard had been replaced, and the new one seemed to be under Johan's command. For that reason alone, Lilo supposed that she should not worry too much about her mother staying there.

They spent only one night in the barn in Krün, Lilo and Bluma tightly wrapped in each other's arms until Lilo would leave, at dawn. Lilo did not sleep one wink during the entire night. She watched the dawn break slowly through the old crack in the boards of the barn walls, a soft rose mist hovering on the horizon. Her mother was sleeping soundly. They had agreed the night before that Bluma would stay in the barn when the bus came. Lilo stole out early, not even kissing her mother for fear of waking her. *Not even a kiss,* she thought. She peered again into the sky. The rosy mist had dissolved into featureless gray. The moon and stars were gone, the sun not up yet. There was only a vast nothingness, as though God were yawning, a huge, abyssal yawn.

When she got to the bus, Django was already there. He took her hand and pressed it to his lips, then led her onto the bus. He said nothing. She blessed him for his silence. He seemed to know that she needed to be alone and sat across the aisle from her. Her hand still felt warm from Django's lips.

• • •

There was one good thing about Sarentino and that was the tents that had been pitched for the extras. Every film slave had his or her own small tent. Lilo's was the tiniest, but it was all hers. Although Lilo missed the warmth of her mother sleeping next to her, she did enjoy sleeping away from the other film slaves. She did not have to hear anybody snoring. The nights were still chilly, but they had good blankets. There were, of course, guards, who patrolled the encampment all night. With the full moon, their shadows stretched across the canvas sides of her tent as they walked by. They all carried two guns, a rifle slung over one shoulder and a pistol in their belt.

There had been pistol- and rifle-carrying guards before. Certainly at Krün, both Johan and Gunther carried firearms, but as Django explained it, the film slaves were now honored with elite guards. These men were no mere local policemen from the Salzburg-Krün region but genuine SS with SS weapons! Django knew a lot about guns from working in a Mauser factory. And being Django, he liked to show off his knowledge. "They say that the Luger, a recoil semiautomatic, had been a seven-millimeter but was redesigned for war. So now it's a nine-millimeter. Most balanced pistol in the world. It is said that the feel of it when it is aimed is as if it is aligning itself with the target. Like it's got a little brain inside it."

"That's awful! Stop talking about it. Why would they

ever need a gun with a brain here on this movie set?" Lilo said with contempt.

"Ha!" Django laughed. "Maybe it's because we're the smartest people on the set."

What he said was funny, but Lilo hated this talk about pistols and rifles.

The crew and film slaves had been brought to this location to shoot two scenes. The first and opening scene would show Pedro killing the wolf that threatened his sheep. The second, which occurred midway through the film, was what Leni called the "romantic mountain idyll." She has run away from Don Sebastian and is found, exhausted, by Pedro. They fall passionately in love and live in perfect harmony in the romantic little shepherd's hut high in the pure mountain air, far from the greed and treachery of the lowlands.

It was rather obvious that the wolf was supposed to represent the wicked and inescapable Don Sebastian. Lilo doubted that anyone had made the connection of the wolf to Adolf Hitler, whom they had heard had recently gone to his military headquarters on the eastern front, the *Wolfsschanze*, or Wolf's Lair.

Since they had arrived in Sarentino, the crew seemed more unguarded in their remarks about the war than before. And talk about the eastern front was rampant. Django had overheard a cameraman saying that troops were very close to the border and action was to begin within not weeks but days.

Django said the Germans were idiots to start action in the east. Fighting a war on two fronts could easily spell doom for them. One could only hope.

But right now the only "front" Leni and her director and cameramen were concerned with was here in the mountains, where the wolf scene was to be shot. They had tried to film this scene two years before and failed. The first time, the animal died. That was when Fanck had stormed off the set and Harald Reinl entered the picture as assistant director. But apparently Herr Reinl had now fallen into at least temporary disfavor, as there was a new assistant director, Mathias Wieman. In addition to Wieman, the other new face was that of a zoologist who specialized in wolves. He had been brought from Berlin. The creature that sat in a cage under the shade of an awning was pathetic. Lilo had seen her share of mangy dogs in the streets of Vienna that looked better than this wolf.

"Now you see, *Liebling.*" Leni was addressing Bernhard Grzimek, the zoologist. "This is really art. Yes, it is a violent scene, but there is beauty at the very heart of it. We must find the harmony." Grzimek looked completely bored but was pretending to be interested. Lilo could tell that Leni wanted art. Grzimek wanted nobody bitten. For Leni the mountains represented all that was good and pure. And in this film they symbolized the opposite of *Tiefland*—the lowlands. Since their arrival, she had blabbed endlessly about the unsullied splendor of the mountains. This was what Lilo and Django had begun here in Sarentino to refer to as Tante Leni's lecture number four.

Again and again she recounted her early movie career, starring in the "mountain films," in which she scaled peaks barefoot. She told all of this with unmatched rapture. And then she would go on to explain how Hitler became obsessed with her when he saw these films. "Ach, the Führer. I think now I have gone with Hitler to his country place, the Berghof, in Bavaria, at least twenty times. He always insists that we watch *The Holy Mountain* together." She glanced over at the cage with the pathetic wolf. "So, *Liebling*"—she took a step closer to the zoologist—"we must find the harmony in this scene. I am fascinated by the beautiful, the strong . . . the healthy."

The flea-bitten wolf swayed on his feet, his tail drooping languidly. Lilo wondered if he had been drugged. Undoubtedly.

"She calls that thing healthy?" Lilo muttered to Django.

"Shush, Lilo. You're going to get us all into trouble. Look what happened to Unku."

"We don't know what happened to Unku. That's the problem."

The conversation with the zoologist was over, and Leni walked away. But then she stopped and scanned the twenty or thirty people, the crew and the extras.

"Where's the girl?"

"What girl?" Wieman said.

"The Gypsy horse girl."

Lilo felt Django give her a poke. She stood up quickly.

"Come here!" Leni motioned to her with her index finger.

"Yes?" Lilo asked as she approached. Franz was standing next to her.

"Let's discuss this riding scene, *Liebling*. You see, if the wolf scene goes well, we shall have time to rehearse the riding scene later today, then to shoot tomorrow." She leaned over and gave Franz a hug and a little peck on the cheek. Rumor had it that Tante Leni had made some headway in her romantic endeavors with Franz. It turned Lilo's stomach to see this display. She understood that he did not want to ski to Russia, but wasn't there something in between skiing to Russia and making love to Leni? It all began to boil up inside of her. She felt like a cauldron of hurt and anger that was perilously close to boiling over. "Any questions?" Leni asked. Franz had his arms draped affectionately around Leni from behind. He was resting his chin on her shoulder.

"Just one," she replied.

"Not about your mama again." Leni laughed softly.

"No, not about Mama," Lilo said, and looked Franz directly in those dazzling blue eyes. "About Unku. Where is Unku?" Lilo could hardly believe she was saying this. It was as if the words came from someone else's mouth. But they were her words, her thoughts, her mouth.

Franz's eyes turned to blue ice. Leni's lips curled back. Lilo noticed again how pointy her teeth were. But Leni said nothing and strode off. Franz, however, was left gape-mouthed, staring at Lilo.

"Why did you ask such a question?" he whispered.

"Because it's not make-believe. It's real, Franz. Unlike your love for Leni, or has that become real?"

"I had no choice."

"No, you're wrong. *We* have no choice. Unku, myself, all of us here." She tipped her head toward the film slaves. "But *you* had a choice." She turned and walked back toward Django.

"What did you do?" Django asked.

"Never mind."

"You did something. She's furious. Look at her." Leni was gesticulating madly as she spoke to Wieman and Grzimek.

"No, they're just talking about the scene." Lilo laughed. "Maybe she's going to turn the wolf on me instead of the sheep."

"Not a funny joke, Lilo."

"I'm just so sick of it, Django," she moaned.

He put his hands on her shoulders and began to shake her. "You can't afford to be sick of it, Lilo." He was absolutely seething. She had never seen him like this. "Do you realize how many others would give anything to be in our place? We have better food than we have ever had since our arrests. For me that is a long time. For you not yet a year. We can hope that when the war is over—"

She shook his hands off her shoulders. "When the war's over, we'll be dead."

The color drained from Django's face. "Why do you say that?"

"Because it's true, Django."

Over his shoulder, she could see Franz motioning her to come. Leni had retreated to her trailer. The zoologist, Grzimek, was talking with his four assistants, who would help him with the wolf. The sheep were being herded to a steep slope.

"Look, Franz wants a word with you, Lilo. Better go."

"What the hell does he want?"

"Just go!" Django gave her a small push.

Franz was looking down at his feet when she walked up.

"Scared the wolf's going to tear you apart?" she asked.

"Yeah, the thought has crossed my mind, but they

gave him a sedative." *God he's dumb,* she thought as she watched him scuff the toe of his boot in the dirt. Should she embarrass him further and tell him that she was not thinking of *that* wolf?

"Uh . . . look, Lilo." It shocked her that he knew not just her name but her nickname. He looked up. His eyes were very sad. "Yeah, I know your name. Unku told me. She said you were her best friend." Lilo felt the threat of tears. "Listen to me. I am saying this for your own good."

"What did you do for Unku's own good?"

"Nothing. I am a coward. I am ashamed."

"Well, I know a quick way you can die if the wolf doesn't get you. You can go to the Russian front. They say the action is starting any day. Won't need your skis yet." She could almost taste the acid as these words rolled off her tongue.

"Fine." He began to speak rapidly. "Listen, if you have to get it out, I understand. I just want to say one thing."

"And what would that be?"

"Go and apologize to Leni. Make it easy on yourself." Lilo shook her head. Franz was at least ten years older than she was. But how could he be so . . . so . . . simpleminded?

"Look, she's very proud. She likes control."

Lilo rolled her eyes. She had given up all pretense of politeness or respect. "As if I don't know that!"

"Look at it this way, Lilo." She didn't understand

why, but she was touched by hearing her name, her nickname.

"What way?" she whispered, sliding her eyes away from him.

"She likes control, but maybe this is a way, through apologizing, that you can get some control."

"Me? Control?" Maybe Franz was not so simpleminded as she thought. She had had no control over anything in so long that it seemed impossible. Was he actually saying she could gain it? Even if it was a small bit, she had to try. Not for her sake but her mother's. "All right. I'll go."

But Lilo wondered if it was control she craved or hope. She felt starved for hope. She began to walk away and then turned back to look at Franz. "Should I just go up to her trailer and knock on her door?" He nodded.

Lilo knew that Leni must be expecting her. She must have put Franz up to this. But still he seemed sincere. Just before she was about to climb the two steps to the trailer, Franz ran up to her and whispered, "I still love her, and I don't know where they took her."

Eighteen

Who's there?"

"Me. The Gypsy horse girl."

"And what might you want?"

"I have come to apologize, Tante Leni." Lilo was flooded with fear. She had to fight an instinct to flee. Her heart was racing. Her breath grew short. She looked around. She heard the roar of the fog machine warming up. Leni wanted fog blowing over the lake. Fake bushes had been "planted," and carpets of real grass had been rolled out on the banks of the lake to make it look more realistic. Salt was scattered around the edges so the sheep would graze in the right spot. But the sheep had become so thirsty that they drank the lake nearly dry. So now Lilo saw the last of the bucket brigade of Sarentino villagers along with film slaves from Krün coming up from

the river to fill the lake. *It is all false.* Lilo thought of nesting dolls. The ones they called *matroyshka* dolls. That was
what her world was like. Except it was not dolls. It was
worlds of fantasy, one within another. Endless fantasy.

Django had overheard Leni speaking to a reporter
who had come to the set the first day to interview her.
"Yes, there is a war going on, but this is my escape." But
was it escape or simply denial? Fantasies within fantasies.
Leni was completely insulated from everything. Nothing
was as it appeared to be.

Just before she knocked on the door of the trailer, Lilo
had thought of the gingerbread house again, from *Hansel
and Gretel.* Lilo could now hear Tante Leni's footsteps,
then the squeak of the door opening.

Suddenly something in Lilo's body commanded her to
relax. A deep composure began to seep through her. Then
it was as if she had stepped out of her own body and felt
herself standing just slightly behind it. Leni opened the
door, and Lilo followed her own body into the trailer. The
next thing she felt was that she was no longer behind her
own body but rather drifting just above it.

She looked down. She seemed to be floating near the
ceiling and was actually watching herself below.

Crumpled onto her knees, the figure that she knew to
be herself was begging.

"Please, please, Tante Leni. I did not mean what I said.

Never. It was wrong. Forgive me." She hardly recognized her own voice. Did it come from her mouth? Her throat? Yet she was perfectly aware that she was still floating, calmly above this nearly hysterical begging figure. *I am kissing Leni's hands!* And yet she did not feel the touch of the skin on her lips. She was numb, but she was conscious of an increasing separation between her two selves.

"I promise. I promise never to say her name again. I know you know what is best for all of us." She was squeezing Leni's hands more tightly. She could see this but not feel it. "But please, please, I beg of you, Tante Leni — protect my mother. Keep her safe. Promise me you will never send her east. She is all I have. You have a mother. I know. I saw her that day when she came to the set in Babelsberg. I know how you love her. I saw the light in your eyes."

"Of course, *Liebling,* of course. Don't worry. When you get back to Krün, you will see that your mama is fine. I promise."

And then in the next moment, Lilo began to sense that she was reuniting with her own body. She felt the floor beneath her knees. She began to stand up, still holding Leni's hands. Lilo could feel the skin. It was sweaty. Leni sweated menace. She dropped the hands instantly and stared dumbly into the close-set predatory eyes. *I begged, but she's an animal.*

By the time she left the trailer, Lilo was completely

exhausted. She asked one of the crew what time it was. She was shocked. Only five minutes at the most had passed since she had entered the trailer.

"Where were you?" Django asked.

"I'll tell you later. What's happening?"

"They're getting ready to do something with the wolf. Not sure what."

Wieman was standing on top of a ladder with a megaphone. "Attention! Attention, please. We are going to shoot this scene as safely as possible. I want the herders to begin driving the sheep over that hillock and down the slope, so that by the time the wolf comes, they will be grazing near the water. Now, herders, crouch low, and as soon as the last of the flock begins the descent—hide. We do not want you in the frame, but we want to get a nice long shot of the sheep coming down to the lake. Is that understood?" He was speaking a strange mixture of German and Italian to half of the dozen or so of the herders who were Italian. The other half were Gypsies from the camp in Krün.

"Look, isn't that Eduard?" Lilo pointed toward a gray-whiskered man. Eduard was one of the oldest of the Gypsy men brought to Krün, but one of the toughest. Lilo hadn't noticed him here until now, though they had been in Sarentino for several days.

"He just came this morning," Django said.

"Well, I'm glad he wasn't brought in for hauling water. He's too old for that."

"Look at him scrambling after that stray."

"I hope I get a chance to ask him about Mama."

There were at least six takes for the sheep's descent. Leni was striding about with her viewfinder lens. *"Liebling,"* she cried out to Wieman. "You see, what I want is when those sheep come down the slope by the rock face there, it should look like a river . . . a river of wool flowing by the rock. It's all about the shades of gray. We want to build up the palette — the dark gray of the rock against the white fleece of the wool." Then she tipped her head back so the viewfinder was pointing toward the sky. "My God, if I could capture those clouds right now. If I could just stop them!"

On the seventh take, Leni managed to capture the clouds for a few seconds, and the sheep beneath them flowed like the rolling river of wool she desired. She was delirious. She kissed everybody, even one of the sheep. The publicity photographer for the film began snapping pictures of her. She played to his lens beautifully as she cavorted about flirtatiously. "You want another picture, Karl?" Leni kissed another sheep. "Is that not adorable!" Her high voice drilled the air.

The wolf in the meantime had been fitted into some sort of invisible harness and was let out of his cage with two handlers, who were guiding him to the top of the slope. The actors were now waiting for the sun to sink farther down. This was to be the shadow shot. Leni wanted the shadow of the wolf to stretch across the same rock face that the sheep had passed. A quiet descended on the set. Four men with rifles, two with pistols, quietly appeared and stood fifty feet from the rock wall. And now everyone's eyes were trained on the wolf. The air was thick with tension, and a chill wind began to blow. Suddenly the wolf did not look so pathetic. His bristling fur was gilded by the low angle of the sunlight. His mouth hung open, revealing sharp, pointed tearing fangs. The animal seemed not simply savage but calculating. He reeked danger.

In the very instant Lilo was wondering how they would get that wolf to go where they wanted him to go, she spied Eduard coming down the slope. Someone directed him to Leni. She couldn't hear what Leni was saying to him, but she pointed toward the wolf and then handed him something. Lilo gasped when she saw the dark drops dripping from the package. *Blood!* It was fresh meat, and the blood appeared black against the backlight of the sun.

"She can't be making him do this," Lilo murmured to Django.

"She is."

"Eduard is bait. He's the lure!"

Albert Benitz, the directory of photography, walked

quickly over to Leni. They began to argue. The wind, however, carried their words away. And neither Lilo nor Django could quite hear what they were saying. She waved him off angrily and pointed to the camera. It was clear that she was ordering him back to work. He shook his head wearily.

A minute later, someone cried, "Action!" Eduard stood just out of camera range with the dripping raw meat. The wolf, suddenly alert, shoved his ears forward and locked his gaze on Eduard.

"Stay! Stay!" Leni shouted at Eduard. "Do not drop it until I say." Eduard was trembling, but he appeared rooted to the spot. "Drop it now!"

He dropped it, started to run, then stumbled. The advancing wolf, his mouth pulled back, revealed his sickle-like fangs in the silhouette against the rocks. Then in a macabre dance, the forms of man and wolf spread across the rock like shadow puppets. Yet there was no sound. For an instant, Lilo thought she had gone deaf. Suddenly a sharp noise split the air, followed by a clamorous popping. She clenched her eyes shut. *The pistol with the little brain inside it,* she thought. And then it ended.

This isn't real. Nothing here is real. She never heard Eduard scream. Never heard the wolf growl. But now people were running all over the set. The first sound was that shrill voice scratching the air. "He's dead! He's dead!"

Leni was shrieking. "The wolf is dead. You shot the goddamn wolf. We have to get a new wolf."

But they would have to get a new lure as well. Eduard was dead, too. The second shot went through the wolf directly into Eduard's heart. This was real. *This is what was at the very center of the last nesting doll. Death.*

Lilo began to lose track of time. The night closed around the film slaves. She heard the guards as they patrolled the encampment. The shadows of their carbine rifles sliced across the canvas of her tent's walls. She wondered what they did with Eduard. Did they bury him somewhere? Maybe with the wolf.

She thought of the strange tricks her body had played when she had gone to Leni's trailer that afternoon—or was it her mind? It was just hours ago, but it seemed like months. There had been that pleasant feeling of floating out of her own body, of so calmly observing that other self below on her knees pleading with Tante Leni. But the rest of her, her essence—or was it her spirit? or soul?— had remained so detached. So peaceful. Perhaps this was what death was like—drifting weightless with only your consciousness for clothing. If she could float and coax her mother to leave her body as well, her thin, wrecked, empty body that had been scooped out by the doctors at Buchenwald, that body must be so light, so buoyant, that it would just rise and drift.

And Eduard—where was he now? She imagined him floating above the mountaintops, hovering in the clouds that Leni had tried to capture. He might be looking down at his own body and that of the wolf as if their physical remains were nothing more than discarded clothes. She could picture them both—the wolf and the old Gypsy man, side by side, loping above, running easily across the clouds.

Death would hurt only for a second. And then you would just slip from your body as you would from a coat that had become too cumbersome. And if you looked back, you would not care about that coat. It was no longer needed. She felt a strange yearning. And as Lilo fell asleep, she prayed that Leni Riefenstahl would never again capture the clouds, not even for one second.

Nineteen

Lilo was dragged into the daylight by a voice outside her tent. It was one of the guards. "You are to report immediately to makeup, horse girl."

They were preparing to shoot another riding scene. The new double they had hired in Babelsberg to stand in for Peter Jacob doubled now for Pedro as well. For the mountain idyll, Pedro and Martha were to gallop across the landscape. Of course it made no sense for Pedro to have a horse. He's a poor shepherd after all. "Shepherds go on foot. They're not cowboys," Django pointed out.

But this was yet another fiction upon a fiction. The *matroyshka* doll was growing fatter and fatter with the fantasies dreamed up by Leni.

Lilo sat in the chair and stared into the mirror. The process to make her a double took longer than the makeup for when she played a street urchin. Although there was never a close-up of her face, they first slathered on the pancake base to lighten her skin to a shade closer to that of Leni's, whose skin they had to darken to make her look Spanish. But not too dark. Nazis did not like their idols too dark. Beneath there always had to be just a hint of the super-race. The Aryan.

"This wig," Bella was saying as she fixed it on Lilo's hair. "I have to make it tighter so it won't slip off. They want you to gallop today. It would look pretty funny if suddenly your hair went flying!" Bella giggled. Lilo remained silent. Bella cocked her head and looked at Lilo in the mirror. "What's wrong, *Kleine Püppchen*?"

Little Poppet, she calls me! It was a common enough term of endearment that an elder might call a young child, and sometimes these terms hung on into adolescence, the way her mother persisted in calling her *Little Mouse*. But she and Bella had no history as a mother and child had. And yet she had used these terms on more than one occasion. Why? Lilo wondered. Just habit? She was not, after all, an endearing child. She was part of a hated race. She was a Gypsy. A prisoner. A film slave.

Lilo wondered why she was suddenly thinking so much about words. Words had become as meaningless as the movie set, where nothing was real. Maybe language was the first thing Hitler had slaughtered. And then the rest just followed. The Bible said that "in the beginning there was the Word . . . and the Word was God." But now, in the end, there were no words, at least not real words. And there was no God, just Hitler and his tin-pot goddess Leni Riefenstahl.

"You've worked on all her movies, haven't you, Bella?" Lilo asked.

"All Fräulein Riefenstahl's?" she asked Lilo's reflection in the mirror, since that is how they conversed in makeup—it was their reflections that did the talking.

"Yes." Lilo's reflection nodded.

"Not all. Most. She likes me. I know her face."

This of course begged a question that Lilo could not ask. *Do you know what is behind that face? Because I do.* Instead she simply said. "You like her?"

"I love her. She is, as Hitler has said, the perfect German woman."

"He said that?"

"Oh, yeah. He's been quoted many times saying that." She nodded at Lilo in the mirror.

"Are they having an affair?"

Bella turned down the corners of her mouth and raised her eyebrows, then shrugged as if to say, "Who's to know?" but instead said, "Let me tell you something, *Schätzchen,* I don't gossip. That's why I get where I do in this business." She reached toward a table with an assortment of earrings. "Let's see which ones for this scene. I think Fräulein said the big hoop ones with the little beads dropping from them. Yes. I'm sure those are the ones."

She fixed them to Lilo's ears. She suddenly looked more like a Gypsy than she ever had in her life. Not a prim Sinti girl but a wild Roma tart. Her mother would have fits if she ever went out like this. Bella reapplied the deep red lipstick. Since it was a black-and-white film, her lips wouldn't look red but black like the drops of blood from the raw meat Eduard had carried. Like the blood that had gushed from his chest.

"There you are, my pet!" Bella exclaimed, and they both stared into the mirror at her reflection. Bella was delighted with her handiwork.

"What did they do with Eduard?" Lilo asked suddenly. The reflection looked stumped.

"Who's Eduard?"

"The Gypsy who was killed yesterday."

"Oh, him. I don't know. But I know what they did with the wolf."

"What?" The earrings trembled in the mirror.

"Skinned him. He'll make a nice muff for someone."

The horse she rode was a sturdy mountain creature from the village of Sarentino. The double for Franz, a fellow named Egon, was a fairly good rider. He and Lilo were supposed to ride across the crest of the hill. They were to begin with a slow trot and then spur the horses on to a gallop. "When you reach the crest, race the clouds!" Leni shouted, throwing back her head. "You are free. The essence of freedom. I want the Gypsy's hair to stream out behind her, unfurling in the wind. You are the wind. You are the pureness of the mountain air. *Free, free, free.*"

Lilo closed her eyes. *I am a captive in an endless nightmare. Behind me is a maniacal woman screaming about freedom.* What would happen, what might really happen, if she did simply ride off? How fast could she get this horse to go? Could she pretend he was running away with her? This could be her chance, her one chance. However, there were the little pistols—the ones with brains, the most balanced pistols in the world that always find their target. But it would hurt only for a second, and then she would slip from her body. *Let them skin me. But I would be free.*

She and Egon were riding up through the meadow toward the crest of the hill. A breeze ruffled the grass through which they were riding. "So, Gypsy girl," Egon said. "You ride a lot. Was it a caravan horse you rode?"

"My family didn't have a caravan. We lived in a flat in Vienna."

"No kidding?"

"No kidding. But maybe we shouldn't talk."

"Why not? They are getting pan shots. We are supposed to look like we are chatting—not just chatting, in love." He leaned over toward her as if to kiss her cheek. A wave of something garlicky radiated from him.

"Look, let's just ride and pretend we're talking." She would have loved to tell him he stank, but instead she was trying to concentrate on this amazing possibility of escape. Sarentino, she knew, was down the slope and to the right. It was the closest village. But it would be such an obvious place to go first. She had no idea of the geography of the region and what else was around. In the distance to the south and east, however, she could see a band of trees. A forest. Through the forest and then what? She tried to picture the map of Italy. Maybe she could ride this horse all the way down the boot of Italy to the coast and then across the sea to Greece. The Germans hadn't gotten to Greece yet. They had tried six months or so before, but the Greeks had pushed them back.

Lilo was suddenly back in the classroom at the Franz Joseph School on Hartigasse in Vienna. Frau Hoffritz was pulling down the map of Europe. She could, in her mind's eye, see the heel of the boot of Italy sticking down into the Adriatic Sea—just a hop, skip, and a jump to Greece. They had learned about ancient Greece, not just the gods and goddesses, not simply the mythology, but Greece as the cradle of democracy—that is what Frau Hoffritz called it. It seemed impossible that fifteen months ago, Lilo had been sitting in Frau Hoffritz's class. She taught them about the playwright Aeschylus, the philosophers Aristotle and Socrates, the historian Herodotus, the scientist Archimedes.

Frau Hoffritz said that not only was Greece the cradle of democracy but that the Greeks invented the idea of human freedoms. "'Be convinced,'" Frau Hoffritz said quoting the Greek historian Thucydides, "'that to be happy means to be free, and that to be free means to be brave.'" *I am bound for Athens!* Lilo dug her heels into the flanks of the horse. *To be free! What a noble thing!*

"Hey, Gypsy girl, you ride too fast!" Lilo had given the horse his head and was streaking across the crest of the hill. In the distance she could see a deep-green valley and the sky pouring into it, offering up a cup of blue. She looked back and saw Egon waving for her to slow down. The camera truck below was honking. She had ridden out of the frame! Yes, out of the frame! She could discard her body like a piece of clothing but not her freedom. *I am happy. I am free. I am brave even if I must die, but . . .*

She suddenly reined in the horse. She could not go on. The thought tore into her with all the force of that nine-millimeter bullet from the Luger. And like the Luger, it had aligned itself perfectly with its target. The memory of her mother in Krün. Instantly Lilo knew that she was bound to this place, this earth, for as long as her mother lived. As long as she had a breath in her body, Lilo could not leave. She could not ride to Athens. She could not slip from her body as Eduard had, or the wolf. She had to go back. She slowed to a walk and turned the horse back. He had broken a sweat and was panting. Lilo felt nothing. Nothing at all.

That night in her tent, she tried not to think of Athens, or Pericles, of Frau Hoffritz, who might be in a camp herself. She was Jewish. It was too sad to think of all that. Oddly enough the only comforting thoughts she had were of the dead—Eduard and the wolf. And so Lilo dreamed of the things left behind. It was a confusing dream, for sometimes she felt as if she were really awake. A soft rain began to fall during the night. Her tent leaked, and the rain fell on her face. She felt the water, so she told herself she could not be dreaming—or could she? She saw something beside her. It was a woman's figure, lying quietly, her chest rising and falling. *I know you,* she thought. Or did she hear her own voice saying it out loud? The figure looked so familiar. "Do I know you?" She laughed softly. "You know me, don't you?" she asked the woman.

But already the figure was beginning to fade. "Don't go . . . don't go." The glow pulsed a bit. "I'm tired, a bit tired," Lilo said. And the figure slipped away into the darkness. And yet where she had lain, the bedding was rumpled and warm as if the body were still there.

KRÜN

Summer 1941

Twenty

The filming had wound down at Sarentino within a week after Lilo had experienced her strange waking dream, and they had headed back to Krün for some final scenes. All she could think about the entire way back was her mother. With each passing mile, she became more agitated. Django sat quietly beside her with his arm around her. Every once in a while, he would squeeze her shoulder.

However, as soon as the bus turned into the farm and pulled up in front of the barn, Lilo knew. She was gone. Her mother was gone. It was as if there was a hole in the air. She didn't even need to go into the barn. She knew it before she even reached the door of the barn. And as if to confirm what she knew, Johan's eyes would not meet hers. She was rooted to the ground, to the mud in the barnyard.

Chickens clucked around her. One pecked at her big toe, which stuck out of her falling-apart shoes. She was aware of a small figure shooing the chickens away.

Then Django came up.

"What's wrong with you?" He stuck his head forward in a movement that bore an uncanny likeness to the chicken that had just been pecking at her toe. But then she saw a soft terror fill his eyes. "Lilo . . . Lilo." There was a hot desperation as he whispered her name.

"She promised, Django. She promised."

"What? Who promised?"

"Tante Leni! Promised she would not send Mama away."

"But . . . but . . . uh . . . she might be here. We only just arrived." He took her hand as if to lead her to the barn, but he couldn't hide that he knew she was right. And the queer thing was that she suddenly felt terrible for Django. She didn't understand why. But she did. She felt almost as bad for Django as she did for herself. She realized in that instant that despite his bravado, his swagger, his bluster, beneath all that, there was a naïveté, or possibly—the thought suddenly struck her—he was not naive at all, but it was his caring for her that made him desperate to believe. She wanted him to believe that they could both walk into that barn and find her mother there, or, if not there, by the fence playing with the kitten that the little girl Liesel would bring over to her.

They entered the barn hand in hand. Was this how Hansel and Gretel looked going into the woods? But this was the very reverse of that story, an inversion. The mother had never cast them out. They were coming to seek her. The shadows of the barn wrapped around them. There were others who had stayed in Krün and did not go to Sarentino, but they would not look at Lilo nor meet her gaze. Django started to walk over to one, an old woman named Valya. Lilo reached out and stopped him. "Don't. Don't ask her." Django shrugged. "I thought I should tell her about Eduard. That's all."

Lilo realized that he was just saying this. He wanted to know what had happened to Bluma Friwald. But Lilo knew what had happened. Leni sent her east, maybe to Auschwitz — it was open for business now — or maybe to Lackenbach. And what did it matter? She knew that her mother had been sent away, and she felt certain that she was already dead. That had been the meaning of her waking dream when the figure appeared by her bed. But she said none of this to Django. "Let it go." That was all Lilo said. He didn't argue.

She craved darkness. She wanted to go to sleep and sleep forever. But tonight was June 22, Midsummer

Night. The longest day of the year. And the light dragged on, holding the dark at bay. She lay curled in the old hay-bale apartment by the wall with the crack in the boards. Outside, there was a burst of raucous whoops.

"What is it? What is it?" Rosa appeared. "I'm frightened," she gasped. In that moment, Lilo realized that she was done being frightened. There was nothing to be frightened of anymore. Django dashed in, his eyes bright with excitement. This was the old Django, she thought. Django the operator, Django the gatherer — beg your pardon, the runner of information, of intelligence.

"The action on the eastern front has started. Hitler has invaded Russia. He crossed the Niemen River. He's on his way to Moscow!" *So why are we supposed to cheer?* Lilo wondered. Apparently the people on the farm were delirious. "Everybody's celebrating. They brought in kegs of beer. It — it's like Oktoberfest in June! I think I can organize some, for us."

"Really?" Rosa asked. "And maybe some food, too?"

"I'll see what I can do about it." Django winked.

Lilo felt relieved. Not for the Germans, not for Hitler. Relieved for Django. He seemed back to his old self. Perhaps *happy* was not the right word, she thought. *Thankful* was better. But still she had no desire to join any celebration. The emptiness in the corner of the barn she and her mother had shared was palpable, like a pocket in the air, a nothingness filled with the shadows of every-thing. She burrowed down in the hay. Not a trace of the scent of her mother. She recalled again the peculiar dream she had before leaving Sarentino. It was a dream, but the figure had seemed so real and the blankets had still held her form, or so Lilo had imagined. Those boundaries between the waking world and the one of dreams had begun to blur, just like those between the world of the movie set and that of reality. But Lilo began to believe that dreams possibly had more substance than the props and facades of a movie set.

She heard the revelry outside. She was the only one left in the barn. The doors had been left open. Apparently they were allowing the film slaves to mingle in the barn-yard with the farmer's family and neighbors.

"You should come out, Lilo." It was Rosa, who bent over and shook her shoulder. "They have set up a pic-nic table with food and beer. It's . . . it's . . ." Her voice dwindled away, and she gave her shoulder a gentle pat.

Lilo said nothing and just pretended to sleep.

The darkness seemed never to come. The daylight clung. The noise increased. She was grateful that Django did not come and try to rouse her. He would never say it was fun, not to her. He knew, or rather knew Lilo as no one else did in this place, no one else on earth who was still alive. For she was certain that the people who had really known her were all dead. Her mother, her father, Uncle Andreas. She knew it. However, she realized that it was a great comfort to understand that someone still knew her so well. But how well did Django really know her? Her eyes opened wide. *Does he know that I would leave? Is this not the perfect time to leave, to escape under the cover of daylight when everyone is celebrating?* Who would know if she left? Her mother was gone, her father was gone, and perhaps her heart had contracted so now there was only herself left to worry about. This would be her only luxury. Herself! *Don't think of Django. This is as safe as it will ever be!*

Immediately she got up and climbed the ladder to the hayloft where Unku once slept. It gave her a good vantage point so she could observe the scene and figure out just how she would slip away.

All the people were thronged around the table, and at each end, a keg of beer had been set up. It was an odd scene with the extras in their ragged clothes mingling with the farmer's family, neighbors, the farmworkers, and, of course, the guards in their nice clothes. And yet, it could have been any typical midsummer, or *Sommerwende* celebration. Just outside the barnyard there was a clear path to the wood piled up and strewn with flowers and herbs for the traditional midsummer bonfire. She could see that children from the village of Krün were already practicing jumping over the unlit fire. She scanned the faces for Liesel. *She should be over there with the other children,* she thought. But she didn't see her, at least not at first. Then Lilo spotted her—a small, hunched figure almost indistinguishable against the dark trunk of the tree. What was she doing there? Why was she staring—just staring— at the barn?

Then Liesel jerked. *She sees me!* The child pointed to something near the tree where she stood. But she was not simply pointing; she was beckoning. It was as if she said the words out loud: "Come here! Come here and never go back."

NOWHERE

1941

Twenty-one

Run, run, run as fast as you can.
You'll never catch me—I'm the gingerbread man.
I ran from the baker and from his wife, too.
You'll never catch me, not any of you.

Lilo streaked around the fringes of the forest near the clearing where the bonfire was to be lit. At the base of a towering spruce tree was a perfect pair of shoes. Liesel must have stolen them from the children who had set their shoes aside before wading in the creek and practicing their leaps on this hot summer night. But Liesel had vanished.

She wasn't sure how long she ran the first night, because the sun never set. There was no way to mark the passage of time. She passed on the outskirts of many villages and in every one, people were celebrating Midsummer's Night and were drunk on visions of Hitler invading Russia. She even caught the shreds of song—the tune of the old favorite "Watch on the Rhine." People were now singing about the river Niemen, which would have to be crossed on the march to Moscow.

A call roars like thunderbolt,
like clashing swords and splashing waves:
To the Niemen, the Niemen, to Moscow.

The people never noticed her. They were too drunk, too carefree, too enthralled with the chimera of victory on the eastern front. And she was rapt with her own dream of freedom. It was not a dream, however. She was free. The thud of every footfall confirmed her liberation. If her feet had been bells, they would have chimed her freedom.

Once again she had the strange experience of being outside her own body. Running, seeing it stretch out before her. But she kept up. She was not sure how. But when she looked down, her feet were a blur. Even blurred, however, there was a moment when she looked down and saw that her shoes were not the ragtag scraps that she had worn for the better part of a year. Moreover, she was wearing socks—sturdy brown socks.

Then piece by piece it came back to her as she ran. First there was the image of Liesel shooing the chickens away from her dirt-encrusted toes that stuck out from the threadbare shoes when she had returned from Sarentino to Krün. Then the shoes that Liesel with her huge devouring eyes had nodded toward when she had caught sight of Lilo framed in the loft opening of the barn. She was stunned at the little girl's bravery, but she did not pause to even wonder why Liesel had done this, or what it would mean for her if she had been caught. She only ran. It was as if every drop of blood her heart pumped had been distilled to serve this sleek mindless running machine. She was not aware of hunger, of fatigue, of sore muscles. If she had thoughts, they flew from her head as swiftly as the ground passed beneath her feet.

Eventually she did begin to take short rests, always far from any village. But even for these brief respites, her mind seemed bereft of any thoughts except running. Running and keeping out of sight. Life became very simple, a beautiful simplicity, and she felt she could go on forever. If she had been a book or a diary, these first few days would have been blank pages — utterly empty.

Gradually, however, she began to realize that there was another vacancy as blank as the "pages" of her mind. The countryside, the villages, were unusually empty. The gardens that she sometimes stole from in the middle of the night were stripped. Tomatoes had been picked before they ripened, cabbages harvested before they had had a chance to grow to a normal size. Beets had been dug up when they were still the size of grapes, and carrots when they were no bigger than a baby's finger. It finally dawned on her. The villages were empty because all of the men had gone to fight on the eastern front and they had taken what food they could, since an army could not travel on an empty stomach. New crops were being planted where the old ones had hardly had time to mature. But there were no men or young boys to hoe, sow, or plow. That work was now done by women and girls and young children from what seemed like ghost villages.

She began stealing clothes from clotheslines for warmth during the nights, or what passed for night on these long, light days. Still she did not want to weigh herself down. It was all she could do to resist snatching a quilt for a covering, but she knew she should not sleep in the long twilight of these summer nights but keep running, because that was when the others slept and there would be far less activity. She became quite creative when it came to stealing food. Slyer than a fox, she managed to steal into chicken houses just before dawn to wrest an egg or sometimes two from a nest. She learned to eat them raw and soon grew used to the odd taste.

One morning just before dawn, she had slipped into a chicken house and was just reaching for an egg when a young boy, not more than six years old, appeared. He gasped and was about to shriek.

"Don't!" she hissed, and jumped on him. Her own strength surprised her. She held her hand over his mouth. His pale gray eyes were pried open in terror.

"I am a spy. Do you understand? For the Reich. I am on a secret mission. If you breathe a word to anyone and are discovered, the Gestapo will come. Your mama will be taken away. Your father might die because you betrayed a state secret. Do you have a brother?" He nodded. "He is in the *Wehrmacht*, right?" He nodded again. "You are the little man of the house." A light sparkled in his eyes. She had hit a chord. She guessed he had been told this, as all the males in his family had left the farm to fight. "This is your chance to serve. To be a hero. Now, promise me. Not a word."

He nodded eagerly. Slowly she took her hand from his mouth. He did not scream. He started to speak.

"Shush!"

"I promise. But there is cheese in the cold barrel. Take it." He pointed to a barrel.

She walked over. There was a hunk of cheese wrapped in cloth. She looked at him again.

"Take it!" he urged. "And tell the Führer that Jurgen gave it to you. Jurgen Goetz, son of First Sergeant Othmar Goetz, in the thirty-second panzer division."

She took it and left.

Lilo found the emptiness of the countryside was both comforting and eerie. She had not kept track of time and had no idea how many days or nights she had been running. It was shortly after her encounter with Jurgen Goetz that she looked down at her shoes and saw that a seam had opened up. Could she really have been running so long and so hard as to wear out this perfectly good pair of sturdy shoes? She looked up and saw something. A sign. The first sign she had seen since she had fled Krün. Salzburg, eight kilometers! *This cannot be! It just can't!* She had been running east. Running in the wrong direction! Running toward the eastern front. She had meant to run west, toward the Allies. The birds overhead appeared to stop in flight, suspended in the sky, and the sky — the sky seemed to be collapsing around her.

With the long summer nights, she had ceased to notice where and when the sun rose and set, as it hardly seemed to move. She had run through a timeless space devoid of planets, stars. *Stupid, stupid, stupid girl.* And as if to somehow confirm her stupidity, her worthlessness, through the scrim of tears, she saw her left shoe fall apart as she stood stock-still.

She picked up the pieces of her shoe and limped off the road. There was a meadow sprinkled with flowers and a grove of trees grew at the far edge. She had to get off the road. If she met any soldiers, any convoys, they were definitely going to be Germans. Not French, not British.

Twenty-two

What Heisenberg means when he speaks of the uncertainty principle is simply—"

"Don't say 'simply,' Dieter. There is nothing simple about it."

"All right, then. What he means is this: the more specific a particle's position is, the more vague its speed and direction will be and vice versa."

"Bohr himself said, I believe, that these jumps were nothing like the smooth leaps of a cat."

"Yes, exactly—he spoke of the all-or-nothing, the baffling disappearance of matter from one orbit and an emergence into another—as if Earth, he said, suddenly materialized in Mars's orbit—a sort of Russian roulette— pardon the pun!"

The two men laughed. Lilo, hidden in a thicket, had been listening to the men as they sat in their bathing costumes by the lake at the far edge of the meadow. She had no idea what they were talking about. They were some kind of scientists, that much she had gathered, but the more she listened to them speak, the more resonance their words seemed to have. Was she like some particle oddly and unpredictably jumping about? If only she could have materialized in the orbit of Mars rather than deep in Austria. Was she playing Russian roulette?

But did any of that really matter? Her eyes were fastened on the two men's shoes. If only they would take another swim. The man who had made the pun about Russian roulette had small feet. His shoes would almost fit her, Lilo was sure. *Now, go swimming!* she prayed. And it was as if her words went straight to God's ears, for instantly the two men rose up and stretched.

"Let's go. One more dip."

Lilo held her breath. She waited until they were perhaps six meters from the shore and then crept from her hiding place toward the shoes, which seemed to gleam in the sunlight. Just as her hands touched the leather, another hand clamped down on her shoulder and wrenched her around.

"Stop! You little thief!"

She had been flipped on her back in one swift

movement. Then the man yanked her to her feet. He held her arm tightly. She did not even try to wriggle loose, for in that instant she knew she could not run another step. She collapsed. It was as if all the running had suddenly caught up with her. Every muscle felt shredded with all the miles she had run. It was over.

She must have passed out for a few seconds, but as she lay on the ground she suddenly felt drops of water sprinkling down on her.

"*Mein Gott.* She's just a child."

Lilo opened her eyes.

"Who are you?" said the one named Dieter.

"No one," she mumbled. Her first thought was that the spy ruse was not going to work. She was caught. The hands on her shoulder had let up the pressure, but there was no escaping three grown men.

"B-b-but . . . but where are you from?"

"Nowhere."

"Look, she's skin and bones."

She watched the three men whose faces hung over her. Two of them were crouching down near her. One remained standing. They were confused. Shock and dismay filled their eyes.

"Do you think she escaped from one of the internment camps," said the fellow who was standing. The three of them were in their mid- to late twenties. They were nice-looking, and Lilo wondered why they were not soldiers. Perhaps they were. Two, after all, were in their bathing costumes, but the third, who was not, wore summer linen pants and a pale-yellow shirt, not a uniform. No Nazi insignias were visible.

"Not a camp. A movie."

Now the one who had been standing crouched down closer. "What are you talking about?"

She was not sure why, since there was nothing funny, but she suddenly felt the urge to giggle. "I'm a movie star!" She paused, then added, "Well, not exactly."

The three men exchanged nervous glances. "Is she out of her head?" one asked. That must be why she was giggling, but the next thing she knew, she was crying, making the mewling sounds of a trapped animal.

"No, Bruno. I read about this. Leni Riefenstahl's making a movie—a drama, not a documentary." The man who spoke began to pat Lilo's shoulder. "No need to cry," he said soothingly. *Every need to cry!* she wanted to shout.

"That movie she's been making for years?" Bruno asked.

"Yes, that one. I read that she had been using Gypsies as extras."

"Unbelievable!" the third fellow gasped.

"I just read in the paper that they had been filming in Krün."

Then all three of the men's jaws dropped open. "You came here from Krün!"

It was all very odd, but now she had stopped crying. Emotions batted through her like clouds on a windy day. For some inexplicable reason, she was almost enjoying their attention and admiration. "Krün. You didn't come all the way from Krün, did you?"

She nodded slowly, and a faint smile passed over her face, a dim twinkle began to light her eyes.

"Child, you are not a movie star. You are an Olympian." The man who spoke was the one she thought she had heard them call Frank. He had white-blond hair and very deep-set gray eyes. "Look at her feet. They are bleeding. Look at her shoes."

"Good Christ, no wonder she wanted to steal your shoes, Dieter."

"She's welcome to them. But we have to get her to safety."

Lilo could not quite believe her ears. These men wanted to help her? Could that be right? She tried to raise herself up.

"Take me to the Allies," she gasped.

"The Allies?" All three men looked at her in astonishment.

"Now, just rest here for a minute or so," said Bruno.

Then he turned. "Dieter, get her some food. There's still a sandwich in the rucksack."

"But I have to get to safety . . . to the Allies," Lilo repeated.

Dieter was back in a minute. "A sandwich, and two biscuits, and, here, an apple."

She stared at the sandwich for a good half minute.

"Go ahead," they cajoled. "It won't bite you."

"If I eat, will you take me to the Allies?" she asked. The three men looked at one another, baffled.

"Now, not too much at one time. You know if you haven't eaten for a while, well . . ." Bruno turned to the other two. "Her stomach might not be used to it."

Why are they not answering my question? she thought.

They fussed over her like three mothers over a baby. She took a small nibble. "That a girl." She swallowed the first bite, wiped a crumb from her mouth, and held it in the palm of her hand, staring at it, then looked at the three men. Holding out her hand with the crumb, she spoke so softly that they had to lean in close to hear her. "Am I one of those particles in the universe? Have I jumped, not like a cat, smoothly, but suddenly and into a new orbit— materializing in a new orbit? Am I on Mars? I want to go to the Allies. Please. Safety. Make me jump like the particles."

The three men were stunned. "What is she talking

about?" Dieter said softly. They looked at her, their faces swimming with confusion.

"You should know. You were the ones talking about all this. Not me. You must be scientists," Lilo answered simply.

"But not magicians," Dieter said, and touched her hair lightly.

SALZBURG

1941–1943

Twenty-three

Y ou have to understand. Salzburg is crawling with Gestapo. It's not safe."

"Well, what are we going to do, drive her to the Allied forces?"

"Please!" Lilo said from beneath the blanket they had put her under in the back of the car—although by this time she realized that driving her to the Allies was impossible.

Frank was at the wheel of the car. Dieter was in the passenger seat and Bruno in the backseat. Every now and then, Bruno would bend over and lift the edge of the blanket. "Can you breathe under there?"

"Yes, fine," Lilo would reply.

"Well, she seems to know physics. Maybe we could pass her off as a visiting scholar," Frank joked.

"Is that what they call it?" Lilo's voice piped up. She was now eating the apple.

"Call what? And don't eat too much too fast. Not good for you. Don't want to upset your tummy."

Lilo shook her head under the blanket in disbelief. This truly was the queerest experience she had ever had. But it was real! It was not like the movie set, where everything was fake, contrived. And these three men—Dieter, Frank, Bruno—were so funny. How could they be funny and at the same time so genuinely worried about her? Astonishing!

"Do you call all your talk about orbits and Mars and particles *physics*?"

"Yes," Bruno answered. "We are physicists, here in Salzburg for a conference."

"So you don't have to be soldiers?"

There was an uncomfortable silence. Dieter finally spoke: "We serve but in a different way."

"What do you mean?"

"As scientists, we work on things to help the Reich."

"You mean Hitler and the war?" Lilo said.

"I suppose so," Dieter answered. "We don't really have much choice."

"Don't talk to me about choice," Lilo replied.

"You're wrong there," Bruno answered almost fiercely.

"We do have a choice right now, in this instant. And we have chosen to protect you. And what is most important now is that we get you to safety. Unfortunately Salzburg is not the safest place. But I have been thinking. I have a cousin, Marta, who might be able to help."

Twenty minutes later, they came to a stop. "The marionette theater?" Dieter said.

"Yes, this is where she works."

"She's a puppeteer?" Frank asked.

"Among other things," Bruno replied.

"Let's hope she can pull some strings!" Dieter said without the slightest trace of merriment. Indeed, the three men had become very somber.

"I'll be back in a couple of minutes," Bruno said. He picked up the corner of the blanket. "What is your name?"

"My name?" she searched his eyes.

"Your name, dear."

"Lilian Friwald, but I am called Lilo."

"Lilo, you stay still under this blanket."

"Yes," she whispered.

"Can you believe it?" Dieter said. "Here it is, the middle of the music festival, and you see more swastikas than you can shake a stick at, and the best artists banished — Reinhardt, Toscanini. The whole festival is being sucked into the propaganda machine."

"I heard they are going to ban the word *festival* and call it *Salzburger Theater- und Musiksommer,* Salzburg Summer of Theater and Music."

"What's in a name? as Shakespeare said—crap by any other name would still stink," Frank muttered.

"I thought it was a rose," Lilo whispered.

"You studied Shakespeare, Lilo?" Dieter asked, turning around.

"Once—so long ago, in school in Vienna." The two men grew very still. She heard one of them sigh. She thought it was Dieter.

The car door opened. The edge of the blanket lifted. Luminous gray eyes peered into the darkness. "Don't worry," the woman whispered, and gave Lilo's hand a squeeze. Her skin was quite fair in contrast to her dark, almost-black hair, cut in a short bob that framed her heart-shaped face. "Bruno will take you to my flat, but he will keep you in the car until I get there. It won't be long. He's going to take you in this blanket. Curl up so no one will see your feet. Try and look like a sack of potatoes." She laughed softly.

"All right!" Lilo whispered. She was now for the first time since she had left Krün scared, really scared. These people seemed to care for her. But for so long she had lived in a world of fictions, it was impossible to know what was real and what was not. How did one learn to trust again? Trust was a casualty as much as she was, certainly. Did these three men and the heart-faced lady named Marta really care whether she lived or died? Were they really willing to risk their lives for her—a Gypsy girl? They could all be killed. All sent to the camps to die. It had all seemed so simple when she had been running mindlessly through that void of time and space. But now she had acquired a new encumbrance. The precious burden of good people who might die if they were discovered harboring her. "Don't worry," Marta said again, and ran her fingers through her hair.

Lilo looked at her closely. *Maybe I should worry. Maybe I am being taken into the gingerbread house.*

Lilo was lifted out of the car and slung over Bruno's broad shoulders. Her heart raced. She felt the panic rising like an immense tide within her. What if she jumped from his shoulders and ran? But Frank and Dieter were close behind and on either side. What chance would she have? They said the streets were crawling with Gestapo. She felt Bruno tense. She froze.

"*Heil Hitler!*" Three voices rang out. She slipped a bit as he raised his arm.

"Ah, Herr Doktor Molken. I plan to attend your session tomorrow at the conference."

"I am pleased. I hope you enjoy it, General Graff."

"You should hope I understand it." The general laughed. "Looks like you've got a load there. I shan't detain you."

Lilo could see the jackboots as they passed within inches of her.

Suddenly a glockenspiel rang out. *My God,* Lilo thought, *they're playing Mozart's "Mailied."* Her father had often played this tune at the restaurant in Vienna. It was a favorite accompaniment to bringing in a cake for an anniversary celebration. *But Papa isn't here. This is no celebration. I am a human sack of potatoes, and the streets are filled with Gestapo.* Some more shiny boots walked by. A Gestapo agent? Or another Nazi officer? And all while the din of those crazy chimes rang out the hour from the clock tower. How could two such worlds exist in the same moment—Mozart and the shine of jackboots?

"Two tickets to tonight's performance for *Der Rosenkavalier.* Good seats. Cheap! Come on! Come on! Step right up. Don't let war stop opera. Hans Knappertsbusch conducting—the Führer's favorite conductor!"

Swirling through the air with the glockenspiel music was the sweet scent of *Nockerln,* the puffy pastries heaped with billowing meringues said to celebrate the hills of Salzburg. These had been served in the Café Budapest. Lilo felt as if she were the dark, dirty secret being whisked through some manic celebration. In the car she had thought she had finally encountered reality, but now she wondered if she had merely escaped from one bit of artifice to another. Django's words came back to her: *"Nothing's real here—the village is fake. The Spanish dancer is a Nazi. The shepherd is an Austrian ski instructor. It's all fiction. What's a little bit more?"*

But she wondered, if one were to peel away all the layers of deception, like the skins of an onion, like the shells of the nesting *matroyshka* dolls, what was left? Was she, Lilian Friwald, the last *matroyshka* doll?

Twenty-four

She heard a door open, then a soft voice. "Yes, right into the parlor. Shut the door quickly." Lilo felt herself being set down. The blanket dropped away. Standing in front of her was Marta. She was so tiny, she might have been one of the marionettes from the theater where she worked. But her mouth, which had been half open in shock, suddenly closed. Her lips compressed as she tried to stifle a cry. She walked stiffly forward and then lurched toward Lilo and embraced her.

"Poor child. Poor, poor child. That it has come to this!" she whispered into her ear. She squeezed Lilo's thin arms tightly. "You are like a stick. I shall feed you, bathe you. You are safe here."

Marta backed away from her but still held on to her arms as if she were fearful that Lilo might blow away.

She tilted her head, looking as if she were on the brink of tears. "B-b-b-but," she stammered, "it might be difficult for you because you really are not going to be able to go outside. You can't be seen. No one must know you are here. It's like jail, I'm afraid."

Lilo looked around at the cozy flat. No, not just cozy, but pretty. How long had it been since she had been in a place that was pretty? There were curtains with ruffles and an oriental carpet on the floor. There was the scent of furniture polish. In the living room there was a small chandelier. The prisms cast a shifting embroidery of light on the walls. Oh, it was all so pretty! She turned to Marta and the three men. She smiled slightly. "I've been in worse prisons." She paused. "But why would you do this? This is a huge risk for you."

Marta grew very still. "Doing nothing is a greater risk," she said softly.

That night was the first night Lilo had slept in a real bed with a real mattress since her arrest, almost nine months before. It had clean sheets and a fluffy pillow. Marta sat down on the edge. She took Lilo's hand and began to stroke it gently. "Lilo, you must understand a few things. During the day, when I am gone, you must not ever answer the door or the telephone. And you must always be in your stocking feet, not shoes."

"I have no shoes except the ones I tried to steal from Dieter and Bruno and Frank."

"Ah, yes, that's true. I forgot. But during the day, you had better not run any water for tea or baths or even flush the toilet. You understand, don't you?"

"Of course, Marta." She began to cry softly and turned her head into the pillow. No one must hear her. No one!

Marta rubbed her back. "You poor child." She rubbed her back until Lilo fell asleep.

Their days quickly fell into a routine. Marta would get up close to seven in the morning and make them both breakfast. She always came home for lunch, so they would eat together. Although Marta complained of the shortages, it was the best food Lilo had eaten in months. There was always milk and eggs and heavy cream. Sometimes bacon or sausage and always pastries. Salzburg was nearly as famous as Vienna for its pastries. During the day, Lilo mostly read. She read and she cried, as she could not help thinking about Django. She was careful, however, to not just muffle her tears so the people in the flat below or next door would not hear her but to freshen her face with the water from the pitcher that Marta always left for her to drink. She crept around the flat as quiet as any cat. When Marta returned, they would play some of her records to camouflage their conversation. Still, they kept their voices low.

Marta usually brought a newspaper home with her, and Lilo devoured it for news of the war. One day, however, when Lilo came out from taking a bath in the evening, Marta was stuffing the paper or at least part of it in the trash receptacle. Lilo said nothing. She even pretended not to notice, but she knew there was something Marta did not want her to see in the evening edition of the *Salzburger Nachrichten*. In the morning, Marta always took out the trash. The rules of the building did not permit setting out of trash before seven o'clock. So Lilo waited until Marta was sound asleep and then crept out to the kitchen. She didn't have to dig far into the trash to find the sheet. As soon as she smoothed it out, she saw what Marta had tried to hide from her. The headline leaped out at her. *"Juden im Dachboden des Apotheker Entdeckt,"* "Jews Discovered in Pharmacist's Attic." There was a photograph of the Gestapo leading four people down some front steps. She had just started to read the article when she felt a hand touch her shoulder.

"I didn't want you to see that."

"Of course not," Lilo said hoarsely.

"We agreed from the start that it was a risk. It's a risk I want to take. Don't argue with me."

"I'm not arguing." Lilo felt a sob rising in her throat and reached out and buried her face against Marta's thin chest. "I'm not arguing," she whispered. "Let me cry. Even if I can't cry out loud."

"No one will find you here. Not if we're careful, Lilo. I promise you."

It was a foolish thing to say, as Lilo knew that such promises should not be made, but she did not argue.

The days slipped by slowly. Sometimes Lilo felt as if she were watching sand slide through the most enormous hourglass, one with a ton of sand and a passageway from one end to the other that was perhaps one-thousandth of a millimeter wide. It could be excruciating. And it was those times when she thought of Django. Marta must have noticed Lilo's frustration, because one day after Lilo had been there nearly four months she whirled into the flat and immediately turned on the record player. Her color was high, but it was not just the nip in the late autumn air. She held up the satchel she was carrying.

"You said your mother was a lace maker. Are you any good with a needle and thread?"

"Pretty good," Lilo said. "Why?"

"Here's why!" She dragged a marionette and a bundle of tiny garments from the bag.

"What is it?" Lilo asked.

"A dummy."

"Aren't they all dummies?"

Marta giggled. "Absolutely, but this is a costume dummy. We use it when we have to make completely new costumes. We are not allowed to take the actual marionettes home for fittings. They are too valuable. Would you believe that two were stolen last spring? Probably bartered for something on the black market. In any case, we have a lot of work to do, what with the Christmas season nearly upon us. So we start taking work home. You want to help?"

"Sure."

"Meet the Queen of the Night." She waved the dummy in the air.

"Queen of the Night?"

"A major character in the opera *The Magic Flute.* She needs a complete redo of her costume. So here's the costume." Marta pulled out a midnight-blue velvet gown that was edged with black beading. "You must remove the beading very carefully. We save that for the new gown, and then you will put it back on. You want to try sewing it? I have the pattern right here."

"Sure."

"And I also brought home some decorative materials.

We like to sort of spruce up the design a bit. That way the costumes don't look exactly the same every season. So if you want to get a bit creative, it's all right."

By the time Marta returned from work the following day, Lilo had completed the costume.

"*Mein Gott!*" Marta whispered when she saw the gowned dummy. "It's beautiful. What have you done?"

"Not much, really. Just made a wide inverted pleat in the front and set this lovely black-on-black fabric in it."

"But that's what's so great—the subtle contrast between the midnight-blue and the black fabric. That's the fabric used for the queen's attendants, so now it will all . . . all come together visually so well when they appear onstage."

"Oh, I didn't know that was the fabric of her attendants. I just thought it was nice."

"And then you added that bit of flouncy lace around the neckline. That, too, is sheer genius. The puppeteers love it when the fabric can move a bit and accentuate the motion of the marionettes."

Marta came over and gave Lilo a hug. "Such a shame that I am going to get all the credit."

"Don't worry—it keeps me occupied," Lilo replied.

• • •

And it did occupy her through the Christmas holidays, which she and Marta celebrated quietly together. The day after Christmas, however, Dieter and Bruno and Frank surprised them by bringing a somewhat scrawny goose along with jams, jellies, and an assortment of pickled vegetables from Frank's grandmother. They had even brought Lilo a present—a pretty scarf.

"We thought the color was right for you," Dieter said. They were all quiet for a moment. It was a strained silence, for they were thinking the same thing: *Where will she wear this?*

Bruno suddenly spoke up: "It's a gift of hope, Lilo. Hope and faith that this war will end and you will be able to walk out into the sunshine, a young lady with this scarf tucked smartly in your collar or perhaps like a movie star on your head."

"*Ja!*" Frank boomed. "Like Marlene Dietrich."

"But then we'll have to invest in some sunglasses for you. All the movie stars wear them," Dieter said, and they all laughed, even Lilo.

Thank God they didn't say Leni Riefenstahl! she thought. *And movie stars wear sunglasses so they won't be recognized— just like me, except I'm not a star but a Gypsy.* She said nothing, however. It was so sweet of them. She liked to think of these three young scientists going into a department store, shopping in the ladies' section for something to bring to her for Christmas.

There possibly could be occasion for hope as the German invasion into the Soviet Union had not gone as well as expected. The Red Army had repelled the *Wehrmacht*'s fiercest blow. Nevertheless, she blamed the scarf for making her think more and more about being outside.

The sewing still occupied her, but as winter turned to spring and the days grew longer until it was summer again, Lilo began to brood. When Marta came back one day toward the end of June, she found her sitting holding a needle but absolutely still.

"Lilo. Lilo, are you all right?"

She felt frozen, as if she had suffered some sort of seizure or stroke.

"What is the date?" Lilo asked.

"The date?"

Lilo nodded.

"June 21, 1942."

"It was a year ago that I ran away. It is the longest day of the year." She looked toward the window, which was partway open. There was a pale golden light outside, and the gauzy curtains blew freely.

Marta followed her gaze. "Lilo," she said softly, "it's time for you to go out."

Lilo gasped. "You mean it?"

"I mean it. You've read every book I own, and you can't sit here sewing forever. We'll hide you now under the cover of daylight."

Under the cover of daylight? Is this possible? Lilo was skeptical.

"From now on you are . . . are . . . Christa. Yes, Christa. You are my cousin from Vienna. You were orphaned. Your father died on the front. Your mother of cancer. I am taking you in, as you have no other relatives. You'll work in the shop with me. You see, the Reich has ordered that we send traveling tours to the front of occupied territories. We have one in Norway, two in Poland, and they are preparing a tour to Russia and Romania. We're down to a skeleton crew here at the home theater. We need people. And I certainly know you can sew. I'm going to take you to the marionette theater. You'll blend in with everyone, everything. You'll become part of the landscape — the scenery."

"But look at me. I'm dark like a Gypsy."

"You're not so dark, and your hair — well, I can fix that."

"How?" Lilo asked.

"We'll bleach it. I'm going out right now to get the stuff. And I'm going to buy you a dress."

An hour later, Lilo sat on a stool in the tiny bathroom while Marta applied the bleach to her hair.

"This brush works great, better than the one that came with the bleach. We can get to your roots with this."

My roots, Lilo thought. The word had a strange resonance that had nothing to do with bleaching her hair. Perhaps a shadow crossed Lilo's eye, or her expression changed ever so slightly, but Marta's hand stopped midstroke as if she sensed she had touched a nerve, veered too close. Their eyes met in the mirrored reflection.

"I used to sit like this in the makeup chair for the movie. Bella was her name." This was not what Marta had expected to hear.

"Bella?"

"Bella was the makeup artist. She was good."

"Did she make you pretty?" Marta asked in a hesitant voice. In all the time, almost a year, since Lilo had arrived, she had never really spoken much about her experience in the Gypsy camp or her work on the film for Leni Reifenstahl.

Lilo laughed harshly. "Are you kidding? We were dirty street urchins. They smeared dirt on us. Put sticky stuff in our hair and pulled it into tangles." Then she thought about Unku's bald spot, and tears began to run down her face. Her body heaved. It was as if a dam had broken. She slumped over in the chair and sobbed.

"Don't cry, don't cry! You can't get the bleach in your eye. It will sting like hell. Please, Lilo—Christa . . . don't cry."

Lilo looked up. It was in that moment that she decided to tell Marta about Django.

"I had a friend," she began tentatively. "His name was . . . is . . . Django."

Django! It was the first time she had actually said his name out loud in over a year. It hung in the air like a chime in the twilight. It glimmered like the first star of the evening. "Django," she said again.

Twenty-five

The limp figures dangled in the dimness of the workshop from suspended ceiling racks. They turned slowly in the scattered shafts of light as if in a silent dance with the circulating dust motes. It was a mournful dance, for their heads were dropped forward on their narrow chests. Many were not costumed. They appeared skeletal despite the muslin batting on the frames of their jointed stick bodies. Marta snapped on the overhead lights.

Lilo inhaled sharply. If the movie set of *Tiefland* was strange, this world was even weirder. The "actors," the puppets, with their faces frozen into expressions of mystifying neutrality, were like specters that rose to haunt the world of the living. Lilo felt the skin prickle on the back of her neck. She had goose bumps despite her long sleeves and the warmth of the workshop. Her urge was to run.

But she couldn't. Marta had been so kind. Bruno, Frank, Dieter—they had all risked their lives for her. And outside, the streets were crawling with Gestapo. But inside did not feel safe, not as safe as the flat. There was something profoundly disturbing about the limp figures that evoked notions of mortality, intimations of death. And death, she knew, could be very patient.

"Why do they all have the same expression?" Lilo asked, staring at the serenely bland face of a female puppet. They seemed to have slightly more character than the blank dummy she had worked on when sewing costumes but not much.

"Oh, they aren't all the same. Look at this one," Marta said, unhooking one who had a scowling grimace. "She's the evil witch in the Rapunzel story. There are basically two expressions that we carve. Good and grimace, we sometimes say. That's Rapunzel," she said, pointing at the bland-faced puppet. "And here, the Witch. We basically have one kind of good face but a few more grimaces— since evil can be cruel, or conniving, or scowling. There are slight differences in how the mouth is carved and the eyebrows. We usually have the eyebrows almost meet for a scowl and carve deep lines between the eyes." Marta continued to speak for another minute or two, indicating the many faces of evil. *But does she know,* Lilo thought, *that the face of evil can be bland as well? Bland and so very beautiful.*

"The real expression," Marta continued, "does not come from the face but from how the strings are worked. You have to get the feeling in your fingers. In truth, you only have movement to work with for the best expressions. You have to coax the movements of living human beings from these wooden figures. But now to work. I wanted to get here early so that by the time Uta and the shop director arrive, you will already be sitting at the sewing machine."

"But what will they think? I mean, Marta, they don't know if I'm any good at this."

"Never mind. They are desperate for help. We are down to so few people now. So many men at the front, including Herr Professor Aicher."

"Who is that?"

"Hermann Aicher, the founder of the theater. The master carver. Look, Li—I mean Christa. Normally we have twelve puppeteers. We're down to seven. They have even drafted me to work on the platform. Of course, I do the easiest puppets, which don't require much activity. But since I made them, I am familiar with how they move."

She grabbed a puppet from a wire and took Lilo to the tailor's room, which was just off the room for joinery and metal work. "This is Donna Anna." She held up the puppet. "She's from the opera *Don Giovanni*. Her costume's a mess. It needs to be completely redone, but you have to start with the petticoats."

"The lace on the sleeves is terrible," Lilo said.

Marta's face brightened. "Usually I would advise to begin with the petticoats. But no one has been skilled enough to repair the lace." She dropped her voice. "You are! Remember what you did with the Queen of the Night?" She looked cautiously over her shoulder. "Frau Uta will be so pleased. So why don't you begin with the sleeves? Do you think you can do it?"

"Yes. I'll have to tat it. I doubt you have a lace maker's pillow or bobbins."

"No, we don't."

"It's okay. Tatting will work fine," Lilo said, squinting at the lace trim.

Lilo began to work, and soon she heard people arriving in other parts of the workshop. She had just removed the sleeve and begun the tatting with the smallest embroidery needle she could find when some other women entered the tailor's room.

"I want you all to meet my cousin Christa," she heard Marta say. "Come on, Uta, and you, too, Ina."

Lilo looked up and smiled. She was suddenly very nervous. Would they be able to tell that her hair had been bleached, as well as her eyebrows? She wore the dirndl that Marta had bought for her. But would they think *Gypsy* as soon as they looked at her?

"Hello," she said softly.

"Ah, look, she's repairing the lace sleeve of Donna Anna!" the woman named Uta exclaimed. "How beautiful. Where did you learn how to tat like this?"

She was about to say from her mother, a lace maker, but she realized that she might be giving up too much information. For all she knew, when they were in the camps, they had noted down her mother's profession. "Oh, I just did. I loved sewing for my dolls."

"Well, then, you are in the perfect place." Uta smiled and gave her shoulder a pat. "I hope you will be happy here. We cannot pay you anything, as I explained to Marta. But we do need all the hands and fingers we can get!" She lifted her own hands and waggled her fingers.

It was midday when the puppeteers arrived for the rehearsal of that evening's performance of Mozart's opera *The Magic Flute.* They were the stars, and it was immediately apparent that the star of stars was Sepp Lang. He was extremely handsome and apparently was older than he appeared—he walked with a slight limp, which Marta had earlier explained was due to an injury he had suffered in 1918, toward the end of the Great War. It was hard for Lilo to believe that he was more than forty years old.

"He must have been very young in that war,"

Lilo whispered as she watched the rehearsal later that afternoon.

"A lot of young boys enlisted, especially toward the end, though they were barely old enough. I think he was fifteen or sixteen at the most. He actually lost his leg. And part of the other."

"He has wooden legs now? But he really hardly limps at all," Lilo said.

"Yes, they say that's why he understands the movements of the marionettes." She paused. "He is one in a sense. His left leg he lost entirely. His right leg from the knee down. But he's very musical. You have to be musical to be a master puppeteer."

Marta and Lilo sat in a middle row of the theater, which was empty for the most part, except for the director, who sat in the front row, and Uta, who had placed herself in the very back to monitor the sound level of the recorded music.

Under the proscenium arch of the theater perched the miniature stage. It was difficult for Lilo to judge its actual dimensions. Was it ten feet wide or fifteen, and perhaps half as tall as it was wide? Then just barely above the arch but invisible from her seat was the balustrade or balcony from which the puppeteers operated the marionettes. Right now the puppeteers were visible as the curtain hiding them had not yet been drawn.

"To stage right, please!" Uta called out to Elbetta, who was operating the puppet of Papageno, the bird catcher in the opera. After a few more adjustments, the house lights were dimmed. The curtain concealing the puppeteers was drawn shut, and the music of the overture rose. Lilo blinked in disbelief. Within seconds the world in the theater had changed. The puppets, which moments before had seemed so tiny, suddenly appeared life-size. The stage seemed immense. Size and dimensions had been turned inside out. Lilo felt almost dizzy as a mystical landscape loomed up and a desperate prince, Tamino, raced through the swirling blue mists.

Then from stage right a gilded serpent slithered from the wings and began its pursuit of Tamino. Lilo was riveted. Next the Queen of the Night arrived. The costume she had sewn months before possessed a shimmering darkness. Lilo felt Marta reach out and squeeze her hand. The queen's strings were operated by Anna, one of the artists in the sculpture department. The movement was beautiful—free of gravity, or so it seemed. Lilo loved the way the lace that trimmed the neckline seemed to drift around her shoulders when she moved. The marionettes had a fluid grace and appeared to float even when their feet tapped drily on the stage floor in the quieter sections of the music. Lilo quickly forgot about the mouths that never opened or shut with speech, because their movements were so expressive, so exquisitely delicate, that no facial gestures were needed. The face that she had previously thought of as bland acquired a sudden emotional intensity.

How did this happen? It was as if she had entered a place where none of the known laws of the physical world applied. EAT ME, DRINK ME — the words from *Alice in Wonderland* came back to her as she recalled the magical liquid that Alice had consumed so she could fit through the small door at the bottom of the rabbit hole. Alice then ate the cake that stretched her to an insane height. All the proportions of the world as Lilo knew them were turned inside out. The puppets loomed immense, and she felt minuscule in her seat.

"Stop!" someone yelled. The lights flickered on. The curtain was drawn back from the puppeteers' platform. The handsome prince dangled limply — all two feet of him. His master loomed large above. It had all happened too quickly. Lilo closed her eyes for a moment and thought, *Am I Alice?*

Twenty-six

What do you mean? I can't believe it! Not again!"

"Oh, so sorry, Sepp!" Anna apologized. It always happened this way, Lilo realized after more than a year of working at the theater. Anna, a substitute puppeteer, fouled the strings regularly in rehearsal, but by the time the performance arrived, she was fine. Sepp never raised his voice, really; his expression remained as bland as the face of the marionette he operated, which was usually the hero and seldom a villain, and yet embedded at the very center of his voice was a sneer. Lilo felt it, and she knew Anna did, too.

Lilo had been at the theater for fifteen months. It was hard to believe, but it had been three years almost to the day since she and her mother and father had been arrested and taken to Rossauer Lände police station and jail in

Vienna. Three years! It was September 1943, and she was now eighteen years old. She would have been going into her last year at the Franz Joseph School on Hartigasse. The people at the theater appreciated her skills, but Marta avoided socializing with any of them outside of work. She and Lilo had fallen into a pleasant routine and would still return to the flat for lunch. But just being able to walk outside felt wonderful, and she did often wear the scarf Dieter and Bruno and Frank had given her for Christmas. She continued to read the papers voraciously, as the rumor mills about new labor camps being built continued to proliferate.

"They" was how Marta, in the privacy of the flat, always referred to the Nazis, and "him" or "he" was what she called Hitler. It was a kind of code that Lilo became aware of very quickly. She realized that Bruno, Dieter, and Frank had been using it, too, whenever they would drop in for brief visits. It was their form of resistance—passive resistance, but resistance nonetheless. To name something was to credit it, acknowledge it, give it dignity. To refer to it without a name but just as a pronoun was to mark it as she and her mother had both been marked at Buchenwald.

"My God!" Lilo exclaimed as they walked home from work and stopped at a newsstand. "They're evacuating Berlin!" The headline blared the news. They bought the paper and rushed back to the flat.

"It's just civilians, but still." Lilo made no attempt to muffle her joy.

"Have you read anything about carrots?" Marta asked.

Lilo looked up from the paper. "Carrots? What do carrots have to do with this?"

Marta slid her eyes as if looking for someone. She dropped her voice and leaned over the table where they sat reading the paper.

"Disinformation" she whispered.

"What's that?"

"Bruno told me. The *Luftwaffe* is losing more planes than ever before. Suddenly the Allies seem to be able to pinpoint the location of German planes at night. The British say their pilots have better night vision because they eat more carrots."

"Carrots? I don't understand."

"They say that carrots improve night vision."

"I still don't understand."

"It's disinformation. Bruno thinks the British have developed a technology that has nothing to do with carrots — a system for detecting the presence, location, and even the speed of aircraft. It has something to do with electromagnetic waves. Don't ask me to explain, but it has nothing to do with carrots." She folded her section of the newspaper shut. "Come on. It's time for us to dye your hair again, I think."

"Already?"

"Just the roots."

Lilo sighed. She wondered how long she would have to keep this up. When would it all end? Was it true what Marta had said about the British and this new technology? But how much would they have to blow up before they could stop the war? And who would be left? She thought of Django. Where was he right this minute? What was he doing? She missed him. She missed her mother, but she didn't have to worry about her mother. She was sure her mother was dead. Years before, she had wondered about her father and felt that no one was really dead unless you knew it for sure. She had perhaps tried to trick herself into believing he was still alive somewhere. But the tricks were over. She was certain that Leni had sent her mother to Ravensbruck and that her father had little chance of survival. She had to face facts — there was no time for the dead.

When she did think of her parents, her mother and her father appeared in her imagination like the lifeless jointed bodies of the marionettes, but there were no puppeteers to animate them, breathe life into them.

"Is Sepp married?" Lilo asked suddenly as Marta worked the bleach into the roots of her hair.

Marta laughed. "No, but he has a special friend."

"You mean a girlfriend?"

"Well, a woman. Not a girl. The Baroness von Schenck. She is at least ten years older but still quite beautiful. They often take tea together at the café near the theater we pass."

Marta paused and looked reflectively in the mirror at Lilo. "You know, Lilo, we should think about getting out a little bit more . . . just a little bit. It will look more normal."

Lilo knew what Marta said was right. Even though she was supposedly out and under the cover of daylight, her life essentially consisted of moving from one interior to another, from the tailor's room in the theater to that of Marta's flat. She felt confined to the shadows of life inside as well as outside and never felt free to saunter through the sunshine outside. There were parks she would love to visit, plazas lined with cafés and sweetshops, but for all intents and purposes she might as well be a mole. It was her choice. Marta encouraged her to go out more, but she was simply too frightened. There was too much at risk, not the least of which was Marta. She was haunted by what might happen to Marta if she was discovered to be harboring a Gypsy.

Marta finished with the bleaching. "There you go. Now, sit here for forty minutes, then I'll rinse your hair, and you'll be as blond as ever."

Lilo turned around to face Marta. "How long will this go on, do you think?"

"What do you mean, Christa?" Marta had taken to calling her Christa even at home. It was as if she had never known the name Lilo, and yet every time anyone — Marta or the people at the marionette theater — called her by this name, it caused Lilo to flinch deep inside.

"Will I ever be me again?"

Marta crouched down at Lilo's knees and took both her hands in her own. "You are you. A name doesn't matter."

No! No! she wanted to scream. *I am not me. I am afraid to walk in the sunlight. Every time I speak, I am afraid I might say something that will give me away.* She thought of the people she saw in the theater, not just the men and women who worked there but the people in the audience. The children. Lots of children came to the performances. Normal kids, who had returned to school that fall, but where could she go?

She leaned forward and peered deeply into Marta's gray eyes. "Sometimes I feel I just can't go on with this . . . this ruse . . . this lie. I have lost everyone, and now I am losing me. Don't you understand?"

Marta squeezed her hands again. A scrim of tears made her eyes glimmer. Her chin trembled. "It will end. Someday this war will end, and you will be Lilo again."

Lilo wanted to believe what Marta had just said, but it was that quiver in her chin that gave her away. She was trying to be brave for Lilo's sake. *And I suppose,* she thought, *I must be brave for her sake.*

"Come sit down with us!" It was Sepp at the café that Marta had told her about, and there was a woman sitting beside him. She was elegant, even regal. Her silvery hair was swept back from her broad forehead. She had a flawless complexion, and although she definitely appeared older than Sepp, she had very few wrinkles. Lilo felt Marta slow down.

"We shouldn't," Lilo whispered.

"No, remember our talk the other day? People will become suspicious if I keep you so completely tucked away. You have to join into life a bit more."

But life stumped Lilo. For years now, her life had consisted of either prison or living in a make-believe world of a movie set and now a marionette theater. She no more belonged out here on Mozartplatz sipping tea, eating pastries than . . . *Than what?* she thought. One of the marionettes. It would be a performance, but with no one to manipulate the strings. She would hang there lifelessly at the table.

"C'mon." Marta pulled her along. "This will be easy."

There was a table of middle-aged and older Salzburg

matrons next to the one where they sat with Sepp and Baroness von Schenck. The women were hardly fashionable, unlike the baroness. However, it was not their fashion sense that caught her attention but their ruddy cheeks, stoutness, and exuberant health. She thought of the wasted frame of her own mother. They all seemed dressed too warmly for the mild autumn day in tailored loden jackets and Tyrolean felt hats embellished with tufts of feathers and small pins and badges. Many of them wore knickers, thick stockings, and hiking boots. Most likely they were part of one of the local hiking clubs that flourished in the city. They exuded health and heartiness. This was what she with her bleached short blond braids and cheerful dirndl dress was supposed to grow into — the perfect Austrian hausfrau who after producing a number of babies of Aryan perfection would then go hiking in the mountains — the same mountains that Leni had celebrated in her first films, which served as the perfect expression of the Aryan ideal of lofty heroism and supernatural power.

"Hello, Marta and Christa!" Sepp stood up as they approached the table. "Please join us. This is my friend Baroness von Schenck."

The baroness extended a gloved hand.

"A pleasure," Marta said.

"Yes, a pleasure," Lilo repeated.

"What will you have?" Sepp tipped his head and inquired. There was a slight sparkle in his eyes as he asked. It was the first time Lilo had ever seen him betray any facial expression whatsoever.

Marta ordered cider, and Lilo did the same. *If I just sit here and don't say anything . . . Just smile—no, not even smile. Remember the marionettes—a perfectly bland expression.* If only she could dissolve behind a screen of vapidness, complete vacuity, so that she simply blended in with the surroundings.

Their cider came, along with a plate of delicious pastries. So far things had gone well. Another woman, one of the hikers, joined their table. The conversations centered on the trail that had been restored after last winter's avalanche.

"Have a *Topfenstrudel.*" The baroness passed a small plate to the woman.

"Just a bit, please," the woman said.

"Ah, and the *Linzer Torte,*" the baroness pressed. "It is delightful.

"No, thank you," the hiker replied.

"You don't know what you're missing, Gerta!"

"You know," the hiker said as she swallowed a bite of the strudel, "they say that the really best pastry chefs did come from Czechoslovakia."

"Well, now they're ours!" the baroness exclaimed. Her

green eyes glittered triumphantly. The conversation continued. The baroness's remark was the closest they had come to politics. Mostly it was about the trails restored for summer hiking, the schedule at the theater, the last opera to be performed at the close of the festival. *I am doing well,* Lilo thought, but at the same moment, she felt something pinch her thigh. *What is this? . . . It's a hand, you fool,* she thought. *Sepp Lang is . . .* She could not complete the thought. She had to get out. He was now stroking her thigh and pulling at her dirndl. She had to go. But could she? He was the puppeteer. She had no power. How could she signal Marta that something was wrong? Marta was deeply involved in a conversation with the baroness. What would the baroness think? This had to stop.

"I just remembered. I must get back to the flat, Marta. I promised Inga that I would be there. She is dropping off something for me to sew."

"Inga?"

Inga was their upstairs neighbor, who had a horrid little dog, and neither Marta nor Lilo could stand her.

"Oh, yes!" Marta said, and nodded. "Yes, she did say she was bringing by something for you to mend." Relief swept through Lilo like a freshening breeze. Marta got it.

They were not a block from the café when they dared speak.

"He tried to feel you, eh?"

"Yes."

"Oh, damn, damn, damn. I should have thought of that before we accepted their invitation. Sepp can be . . ." She didn't finish the thought.

"Can be what?"

"Well, you know . . . an annoyance to some young women, but I never thought that he would . . . Well, never mind. You just have to keep out of his way as best you can. I'll try to look out for you. But just stay out of his way. He'll forget about you."

And he did seem to forget about her. He never betrayed a trace of undue interest or chagrin over her abrupt departure from the café that day. The incident itself receded if not completely from her memory at least to the point that Lilo wondered if perhaps it had been accidental.

One evening she was working late long after everyone had left the theater. The lights of the tailor's workshop had been switched off except for the feeble glow of the single table lamp where she sat repairing Snow White's costume for the performance the next day. The puppet was perched on a revolving stand in front of an oval mirror so Lilo could see the hem length as she turned it to check the evenness. She had for perhaps the tenth time wondered if Sepp's advance could have been an accident. And the next moment, she thought how she and Django, whom she seemed to miss more each day, had never touched each other that way. Would she want him to touch her? Would she want to touch him? Maybe kiss him?

She felt a shudder deep within her heart and then grew very still. *I love him. I truly love Django.*

Soon the very air in the tailor's room throbbed with this new awareness that burst upon her like a splash of moonlight on a dark and cloudy night. She set down the small scissors with which she had been snipping a seam from Snow White's gown. He was alive; she just knew it. He was alive and missing her. Loving her. He was aching with a love for her as deep and profound as her own.

"Mirror, mirror on the wall." A voice came out of the shadows. Then an image slid across the small oval mirror that crowded out the one of Snow White. *Sepp!* A hand dropped onto her shoulder. She felt herself being spun around on the swivel chair as he wrapped her in his arms.

"No!" she screamed.

"No one will hear!" His inky blue eyes had dilated in the dim light. He was holding her so tight she could hardly breathe. The thoughts came slowly to Lilo — one by one, like pebbles dropped into a pond. She dared not close her eyes but stared into the dead ones of his bland, expressionless face. Evil did not wear the grimace of Rumplestiltskin demanding the firstborn of the miller's daughter. Nor was it the wicked queen in Snow White. Evil needed no such grimaces, but here it was before her—this soulless being, this iniquitous vagabond, this emissary from a godless world. She was unsure of how the scissors came to be in her hand. She thought she had set them down. But suddenly his mouth pulled into a scream. She jerked away from him. "Goddamn no good cursed German!" But then the vile words that sputtered out loud like an over-boiling cauldron were not German but Roma. Roma! Not even Sinti. "Bengesko nazi," a cursed German. She couldn't stop the cataract of Roma curses. He still held her wrist tightly. She saw realization dawning in his eyes. It was as if she could see the tumblers of his brain like the jewels or workings of a clock turning. *He knows!* She tried to wrench free but felt her knees buckle beneath her. She was on the floor. She saw a bloodstain blossom on his shirt beneath his armpit. But he seemed oblivious to the wound. His eyes were now fastened on her.

"*Zigeuner!*" The word swelled in the dimness of the tailor's room.

He began yelling, "*Versteckt! Versteckt!* You're one of the hidden ones. They're picking them up all over Salzburg. Jews in the attics, and now I guess under the cover of daylight—Gypsies, in our beloved theater! Like vermin!" He locked his arm around her neck, dragged her to the alarm box, and pulled the lever.

She looked down at her shoes and blinked. Perfect

shoes. Perfect for running, she thought minutes later as the Gestapo surrounded her. But it was completely over. *Ganz vorbei.* The two words reverberated in her head, sang through her bloodstream. And oddly she felt no fear. *Ganz vorbei.* Fear was useless. All the fear she had ever known simply leaked out of her. She was hollow, empty. She felt nothing.

Ganz vorbei.

Twenty-seven

She had stabbed Sepp, but it was a superficial wound. He had simply overpowered her and pulled the alarm for the security guard. Within minutes, the Gestapo had arrived. She didn't care. She didn't care about anything except that Marta not be caught. But she knew that was ridiculous. Sepp would surely tell the Gestapo that Marta had been hiding her and that would be the end for Marta. Sepp and the guard were dragging her across the floor. She was as limp as the marionettes that twirled slowly above her, their strings taut on the hangers, their heads lolling to one side waiting for "life." Her life was over.

She was taken directly to a city prison in the local police building, not a camp. She expected to be sent to a camp, but now it had been nearly two weeks since her arrest and nothing had happened. Every time a new prisoner was brought to the women's cell block, she expected to see Marta, but so far they had only brought in prostitutes, drunks, and the occasional thief. The drunks were let out when they were sober. The prostitutes languished a bit longer. Finally, when a guard came around at the beginning of her third week, she got up her nerve to talk to him.

"Why am I here? Why haven't I been sent someplace? A Gypsy camp?" At least if she were sent to a Gypsy camp, her chances of meeting up with Django were greater. The guard merely shrugged and walked off. She heard a snort from behind her. It was the red-headed prostitute who was in for the second time in the two weeks Lilo had been in jail.

"I know why you are here still." She spoke in a low, smoke-scarred voice.

"I suppose I must pay you something to find out. But I have nothing. Nothing at all," Lilo said. She had become acquainted with the prison economy—no one got anything without paying in some way. Cigarettes were a major part of the currency, as was sex.

"No matter, sweetie. It's really not worth anything." She smiled. "It's . . . it's rather humorous, as a matter of fact."

"Humorous?"

"Yes." A huge grin broke across her face. "You are still here because they cannot find your papers."

"Papers? I never had any papers."

"Oh, someplace there are papers but they haven't been found. And they can't exterminate you if they don't have your papers. It's the German way. They have an unnatural obsession with order." She now burst out in loud guffaws. She laughed harder and was soon doubled over on the cot.

An unnatural obsession with order. The words rang in Lilo's mind like the muffled toll of distant bells. She found them oddly hopeful, though not for herself. But for the first time, she began to think that just possibly Germany might lose this war. The Germans had many unnatural obsessions, but could something like this actually be detrimental to their ability to strategize? Between July 1942 and January 1943, the German army had failed miserably in its attempts to take Stalingrad, and Hitler had blamed it on the weather. It became the turning point of the war for the Germans. Had they been looking for papers instead of long underwear?

There was one small window in the cell that looked out on an exercise yard. Snow was beginning to fall. It was mid-October. She had been in prison for six weeks. This was still a bit early for snow. But apparently in Russia, winter was coming early.

• • •

It was nearly two months later that a guard came to fetch her. She was driven to a train station several miles outside Salzburg. It was really not a proper station at all but just a stop. A bitter cold wind was blowing. There were other prisoners, she was not sure from where, who were standing on what appeared to be a makeshift platform. Shortly a train pulled in from the east. The doors of the freight cars were opened, and the guards shouted orders for them to enter. The cars were packed. Packed, it seemed, with Russians and Poles. There was a mélange of languages. Most of the prisoners were women and children. A mother held a child of about three or four on her lap. She nodded toward Lilo, indicating that there might be space next to her. Lilo squashed in. She turned to her to thank her. *"Danke,"* she whispered. The woman smiled ever so slightly.

"Sprechen Sie Deutsch?" Lilo asked. Do you speak German?

"Ein wenig," the woman replied, and pinched her thumb and forefinger together, indicating "just a bit."

"Where are we going?" Lilo asked.

"Hölle," the woman replied.

Hell.

RAVENSBRUCK

December 1943

Twenty-eight

Marta is free. Not Marta's fault." Her eyes felt stuck, but she could feel a light so bright that even with them shut, she was aware of the pink lining of her lids — a garish pink, speckled with dancing dots.

"Marta? Who's Marta? This one is blabbing about Marta."

Shut up, Lilo commanded herself. She can't give away Marta. Marta was all she had thought about since her arrest. Would they arrest Marta?

"Where am I?" she whispered hoarsely.

"Recovery," someone whispered. It was a gentler voice. "I'll take care of this one."

Was it Good Matron? Could she be back in Buchenwald? There was something familiar in that voice.

"Open your eyes, Lilo. They're gone."

She clenched her eyes shut even tighter. She did not want to wake up. "Where am I?" Then she felt a wave of nausea and began to gag. Someone lifted her shoulders, and a flood of vomit filled her mouth. Luckily the person was holding a bowl.

"Are you done?"

Now she opened her eyes. "Zorinda?"

"Yeah. Welcome to Ravensbruck."

"They . . . they . . . they did it to me." And another thought crowded her brain. *This is where my mother died. I know it. I know it.*

Zorinda nodded solemnly. "But they did it to me, too, and look, I'm alive."

"For what?" Lilo asked, and gave a laugh, which despite her weakness sounded harsh. "You were right, Zorinda."

"Right about what?"

"You said we should be so lucky."

Zorinda looked momentarily confused. Then a smile broke across her face. "Oh, the chapter when Huck left the Grangerfords and met up again with Jim and they get back on the raft."

"Yeah, you remember."

"I do . . . I do. Now, listen to me. You have to do everything I say. I survived the operation. Now I work as kind of a nurse assistant. Not one girl I've worked on has gotten an infection. I'm good at keeping you clean and all that. But better yet, I can organize food."

Lilo shut her eyes tight, but tears squeezed out at the mention of organizing food. Her thoughts instantly turned to Django. What did she care about food? Django was all she had left to care about. Where was he now? What had they done to him?

"I don't want to live."

"You do want to live! You have to live."

"Why? What for? Everything has been taken from me. They have hollowed me out. I am empty."

"Don't argue with me."

"I'm not arguing."

"Look, you don't want to die of an infection. It's horribly painful."

"I don't care."

"Yes, you do. Let me tell you something." She crouched down close to her head and cupped her hand over Lilo's ear.

"They're losing in the Soviet Union—losing bad. We just have to hang on. American troops landed in Ireland last year. They have established bases in England now. Some say they are going to cross the Channel and invade. And by then the Russians will come in from the east. There's hope. You're going to eat. You're going to do everything I tell you. I am risking my life for you to get you this food. To make you strong. Because when they come you'll be ready."

"Ready for what?"

"Ready to be free."

"I have to tell you something, Zorinda." Lilo's voice grew weak. She paused to gather strength. "I met a boy, a boy when I was in the first camp, Buchenwald. It's a long story, but we were together then in Maxglan, and, well, I fell in love. I don't know where he is, I don't know if he is still alive. I can't explain it. I know my mother is dead. Same with my father. It sort of came to me in a dream, but so far . . . well, not with Django."

"Django — is that his name? Like the musician Django Reinhardt?"

"Yes, but not *the* musician."

"I think he'd be a bit old for you." Zorinda gave a soft chuckle.

"Yes." Lilo smiled. "But this Django is also a very good musician. A guitarist." It felt good to talk about him with Zorinda.

"Then you have to live, Lilo. Don't you see it? If you don't live, it's like killing hope, your hope for him to be alive. Would you want him to wish himself dead?"

The idea shocked her. "No, never!" Her eyes were wide with horror. "Never!"

. . .

Lilo was in recovery for two days. During those two days, Zorinda brought her food and not scraps. Good food.

"Where do you get this?" Lilo said as she chewed on a hunk of bread with some ham.

"There's an inmate. Very educated woman, a metal engineer. They release her every day to go work at the Siemens factory. They make something called the V-2 rockets there and munitions, you know. She brings back food for us."

"Just for us?"

"No, for a few of us. But there are others who work there as well. They are able to get food, too. We have to get you strong really fast. I'm telling the overseer for our barracks that you are ready for work detail tomorrow."

"What's the work?"

"Making socks for the soldiers. I work there, too, on the days I am not in the surgery." Zorinda smiled. Her dark eyes, which tilted slightly, got the most mischievous sparkle. "We make them thin in the toes and the heels so they wear out and give the soldiers sore feet. A little trick."

"How do you do that? A sock is a sock. You just sew it or knit it."

"Not here. The socks are made on machines. There's a way we can set the machines to do our dirty work. No one ever notices. They are only concerned with us making our quota for the day." *An unnatural obsession with order.* The words tolled again in her head.

"Lilo . . ." Zorinda lowered her voice even more. "Things are happening. The word is they want to march us north to another camp. They are worried about the Russians. We aren't that far from Russia here. Not really. If they cross the Oder, the Rhine, East Prussia will fall. That's why you have to be strong, because they'll march us north when the Russians come."

"North? How soon?"

"I'm not sure, but when it does happen, it's our chance, Lilo . . . our . . . our . . . Mississippi."

Lilo closed her eyes. She tried to imagine running as she had before. Could her legs ever be that strong again? Could her feet be so fast? So swift? They said it was a march, but if there was a chance to run away, could she do it? Could she and Zorinda do it together? *Miteinander?* Life became so complicated. Every time you thought it was just you, only you left, another came along. She looked at Zorinda and put her hand on her shoulder.

"I am strong."

LANDSBERG

March 1945

Twenty-nine

But it would not happen for more than a year, and when it did, it was not a march, as Zorinda had thought. It was not anything like the Mississippi. First, it was just another transport train, this time to Landsberg, a subcamp of Dachau. They arrived in January 1945. For the first few weeks they were there, both Zorinda and Lilo were taken each day with a handful of the healthy prisoners to work at a Siemens plant. They were thrilled, as this was where they could get news.

In the textile factory back in Ravensbruck, making socks, they had first heard that the Allies had successfully landed on the beaches of Normandy. During their first week at Siemens, while winding thin-coated wires on spools for electrical motors, they heard that the Russians had liberated Auschwitz. Then just a few days later, the

Red Army had crossed the Oder River and was said to be within fifty miles of Berlin. By March, word had come that the Americans had begun crossing the Rhine into Germany. And that was when their work at Siemens stopped. Completely.

"It's not good," Zorinda said two days after their work at the factory had halted. "They don't want us going back to work. They're losing the war, and they don't want us to find out about it."

Lilo knew Zorinda was right. What the commandants of the camps feared most was that their prisoners, despite their horrendous physical condition, would take heart and find the energy and the strength to rise up. "But that is the good news," Zorinda added after a moment.

"Wait, I thought you said it was not good news."

"Mississippi—our Mississippi!" Her eyes danced with delight.

"You mean a march like the one we hoped for?"

"Yeah. They'll want to get us out and not leave a trace behind. Just you wait. Our chance will come again. The Allies are getting closer. The Nazis will march us north."

At that moment, a barrage of shots cracked the air. They grabbed each other's hand.

"You're right," Lilo said. "They don't want anyone left behind to tell what's gone on here when the Allies come."

• • •

For three days, there were selections nearly every morning and often in the evening to weed out the weak and kill them before the remaining prisoners marched north. Lilo and Zorinda teetered on a strange border between fear and hope. Fear that they would be in the next selection but hope that the Allies were advancing.

Late in the evening of the fourth day, there was one more selection, but this time the guards did not even bother to take the bodies to the crematorium. They were left on a pile of fresh corpses from an earlier selection that day. Then there was the roar of engines as eight SS men entered the camp on motorcycles.

Zorinda went to the barracks window. "It's about to begin—the march."

Lilo looked at her and then at the immense pile of dead bodies near the selection ground. "We have to get out there."

"Where?"

"That pile of bodies."

"What are you talking about?"

"We're not going," Lilo said firmly.

"What! Have you gone crazy?"

"Not at all." Lilo was thinking how those long years ago she had hidden in a pile of pig feces and escaped the sterilization operation. Well, too late for that now, but she still had her life and hiding in the refuse of death might save them.

"Listen to me, Zorinda. On this march, there will be guards all along the way. They'll shoot anyone who's not moving fast enough. If we can find any chance to get away and run, we'll be lucky. But that's just a chance. If we stay here, hidden beneath that mountain of death, we'll be safe. Do you understand? Safe without having to move an inch."

Zorinda shut her eyes for what seemed forever. There was a static bleating over the loudspeaker. "All prisoners assemble to march in Workshop Square."

"This is our chance. Workshop Square. The lights will be on there. The rest of the camp is dark."

Hundreds of prisoners began pouring out of the barracks to assemble in the square.

"This way!" Zorinda hissed. She knew the lay of the land much better than Lilo. They slid between the shadows of buildings. They could hear the chaos in the square as the warden's shrill voice seared the night. Occasionally there was the crack of a pistol. Another prisoner shot dead, deemed too weak to march. Lights went on in all the barracks as SS men searched for any who had lingered. But ahead, a mere fifty meters from where Lilo and Zorinda crouched in the shadows, loomed the mountain of the dead.

"Now!" Lilo hissed, and they sprinted across the flagstones. She sprang for the pile. There was a soft thud. She shoved bodies aside and then burrowed down. She could hear Zorinda nearby.

"You here?" Zorinda asked.

"Somewhere," she answered.

"Let's hold hands."

Lilo reached out. There was a hand but it was that of a dead woman. Thin and bony and very stiff. Lilo's fingers swept over the face of another dead person, then a breast, and she felt the cavity where the bullet had torn away half the chest.

"Here! Here!" Zorinda whispered. And finally their fingers touched and intertwined. They heard the sound of the motorcycles and a few jeeps. Cutting through the noise of the vehicles were the commands barked through a bullhorn, punctuated by the occasional gunshot when another prisoner was deemed too weak to walk as they were herded like cattle onto the road.

Then at last, a quiet descended on the camp. They could still hear the occasional boom of the artillery and the sound of planes overhead. But toward dawn, the two girls fell asleep, their fingers intertwined.

When Lilo woke, she heard someone gagging and then the sound of vomit hitting the paving stones.

There was a strange garble of words.

"What the hell!"

They didn't really understand the words, but they knew it was English. That much they did understand. Lilo felt Zorinda squeeze her hand.

"English!" Zorinda whispered.

"I know!" Then there were other voices. Some spoke French. French! The Allies were here! Not phantoms but real. They began to squirm themselves loose from the wreckage of death and the shameful pile of skin and bones.

It was Zorinda who first staggered out.

"What?" A black man lowered his gun and wavered a bit. Then Lilo appeared. Three other soldiers came up. They looked in disbelief at the two girls.

"Wh-what . . . ?" the black man was stammering.

"They're alive." Lilo and Zorinda looked at each other.

"You speak English?" the black man said.

"Little bit," Zorinda replied.

"Get Bill. He speaks German—bring him here fast." He looked now at the two girls and began pulling things from his rucksack. "Here . . . here, have some candy, and I got a Hershey bar in here someplace and coffee in this thermos."

They each took a swallow from the soldier's thermos. He unwrapped the Hershey bar, broke it in two, and handed each a half. Lilo took a bite of the chocolate and closed her eyes. It melted in her mouth. It was the most delicious thing she had ever tasted. Another soldier arrived. He began speaking German. "You all right, ma'am?" Her eyes were still closed, but she nodded. *Ma'am—he called me ma'am,* Lilo thought. But that is what she was, of course. She had lost her childhood. Almost five years it had been. She was almost twenty years old. She was a woman, although they had scraped out the innards that had defined her as one. *But I am still a woman,* she thought fiercely.

She felt an energy flow into her. *If I keep eating, if I grow strong, I . . . But no more running as fast as I can. No more. The gingerbread man can stop. The race is over, but the search begins. I . . . can organize . . . my love.* Django's face loomed in her mind.

I'll find him, Lilo thought, and took another bite of chocolate. *I'll find him.*

AUTHOR'S NOTE

The Extra is a work of historical fiction. It is fiction, but it is rooted in history and based on a true story. It is a Holocaust story, but one that has for the most part slipped between the cracks of history. It is the story of two people, one real and one fictionalized: Leni Riefenstahl, a real person who rose to prominence during the early 1930s as Hitler's favorite filmmaker, and Lilian Friwald, a fictional Gypsy girl who became Riefenstahl's stunt double in the making of the film *Tiefland*.

As a writer of historical fiction, I work within a tradition in which facts are used and at the same time altered slightly. I would like to be as clear as possible as to the changes I have made. Most of these alterations have to do with dates or time elements. Despite the wealth of material on the Holocaust and the Gypsy internment camps, there is a lack of detailed source material concerning the timeline of certain events, especially the filming schedule of *Tiefland*. It is debatable when precisely the filming began in Italy, but it was sometime between 1941 and 1942. Although sources indicate that all of the film slaves from Krün were transported east, I have, for the purposes of my story, left some behind. In addition, the jail at Rossauer Lände in Vienna did not open until a few months after the time indicated in this story. And finally, the term *porajmos*, which means "devouring" in several dialects of the Romani language, did not come into common usage for genocide of the Gypsy people until years later. I have tried to remain faithful to the historical period in which all these events occurred. I did not alter dates of small details to subvert history but rather to serve the purpose of storytelling. It would not be good storytelling if the essential fabric of the historical period was sacrificed in the process.

Before she became a documentary filmmaker, Leni Riefenstahl was a dancer and an actress. In her early acting career, she was known for a series of movies called "The Mountain Films." These movies were romantic epics that celebrated the rugged landscape of the Tyrol and Dolomites mountain ranges, with their lofty noble peaks. Her career path had been set as the gorgeous star of these movies until she moved to the other side of the camera and began directing documentary films celebrating Hitler's Third Reich. Her landmark documentary, *Triumph of the Will*, chronicles the 1934 Nazi Party Congress in Nuremberg, which was attended by more than 700,000 Nazi supporters. It is undeniably one of the most brilliant documentaries of the twentieth century.

Shortly after this, Riefenstahl decided to produce, direct, and star in a dramatic feature film based on a Spanish folk opera, *Tiefland*, which tells the story of a beautiful Spanish dancer who falls in love with a handsome shepherd. Riefenstahl planned to begin production in Spain. However, because of the Spanish Civil War, filming could not begin until almost five years later, and by then World War II had already started. Financially underwritten by the Third Reich, production on the film began in Germany in 1940. Since there were no Spanish people in Germany, Riefenstahl decided to use Gypsies as extras and stand-ins. She had a ready source of Gypsies, as they had been rounded up along with Jews and homosexuals and put in internment camps.

Riefenstahl was prepared to do everything in this movie, from writing the screenplay to directing and starring in it, but there was one thing she could not do and that was ride a horse. A Gypsy girl who was an excellent rider was drafted. Anna Blach, a teenager, was assigned to stand in for Riefenstahl during the riding scenes. So it is upon Anna Blach that I have loosely based the character of Lilian Friwald.

In 1935, the Nuremberg Laws, which included policies concerning racial purity, were passed. Among the first victims of those laws were the Romani people, or Gypsies, as they were more commonly called. Not only did these laws restrict the civil liberties of the Romani people, but they also allowed for the practices of the Racial Hygiene and Demographic Biology Research Unit, which, under the guise of scientific exploration, carried out medical procedures on the Gypsies. Supposedly the data would help formulate new Gypsy laws that would, like the "Final Solution" for Jews, help resolve the "Gypsy Question," or *Zigeunerfrage* (*Zigeuner* being the German word for Gypsy). In short, the Nazis were searching for a legal method to incarcerate Gypsies. The question was how to do it.

It took some time for these practices to spread east to Austria, where Anna Blach and her fictional counterpart, Lilian Friwald, lived. And it was not until the late summer of 1940, two years after Germany's annexation of Austria, that census and documentation procedures such as fingerprinting began in Vienna, threatening families like the Blachs and Friwalds.

There were several internment camps that were dedicated to the incarceration of Gypsies. Riefenstahl made her first selection of Gypsy inmates from one called Maxglan. As Jürgen Trimborn writes in his biography of her (*Leni Riefenstahl: A Life,* Faber & Faber, 2007), "Riefenstahl not only had the power to have people released from concentration camps but could also arrange to have them sent there." Many of the Gypsies Riefenstahl chose tried to bargain with her by asking that a relative not be sent on a transport east to where the new death camps, Auschwitz and Birkenau, were being constructed. Anna Blach was one of these Gypsies. She requested that her six siblings be released from concentration camps. In fact, one was but was then promptly rearrested. Upon the conclusion of her work on the movie, Anna was sent to Auschwitz and was the only one of her family to survive the Holocaust. Rosa Winter was another extra. According to Jürgen Trimborn, when Rosa found out that her mother was to be sent from Maxglan to a distant concentration camp, she escaped from the *Tiefland* set in an attempt to see her mother before she left. Rosa was captured and sent to prison in Salzburg, where Riefenstahl visited her. Riefenstahl apparently anticipated a touching scene of apology and forgiveness, but when the young Gypsy proved too proud for that, Riefenstahl had her sent to Ravensbruck. Like Anna Blach, Rosa was the sole member of her family to survive the war.

In December 1948, Leni Riefenstahl was brought before the first of four tribunals that attempted to determine if and to what extent she had supported and profited by the Nazi regime. It was before the second of these hearings that an illustrated German magazine *Revue* published the scandalous stories of the film slaves. Riefenstahl consistently lied throughout the proceedings. Yet at the time, there was not enough evidence to convict her. In 1949, in another tribunal, she was found to be a "follower" of Hitler, but this finding did not warrant her incarceration.

Perhaps one of the people most knowledgeable about the

film slaves was Nina Gladitz, a documentary filmmaker who in the 1980s contacted some of the surviving Gypsies who had been extras on the film. She made a documentary called *Time of Darkness and Silence*. Leni Riefenstahl sued Gladitz and managed to have the film taken off the market and made completely unavailable. At the time of writing this book, the film was in a vault controlled by the Riefenstahl estate.

Leni Riefenstahl not only survived but thrived. She was the master of reinvention. She became an excellent still photographer. She wrote several photography books and made films on the Nubian people. She learned how to scuba dive when she was in her seventies and became an excellent underwater photographer. She lived to be 101 years old and at the time of her death, in 2003, was in a relationship with a man more than forty years her junior. It is disturbing that in the early 1970s Leni Riefenstahl was celebrated by many distinguished feminists as a shining example of women's rights. In the opinion of this author, this was truly a misinterpretation of what it means to be a feminist.

I would like to add a final word about the Gypsies, or the Romani people. Within the population of Romani, there are different groups. Two major eastern European groups are the Roma and the Sinti. They speak different languages. The Sinti speak Sinti Manouche, while the Roma people speak Rom. Generally the Sinti are less nomadic than the Roma and by the 1920s lived in cities and worked as craftsmen and small shopkeepers. The Roma were known for their musical abilities, and they often worked as circus-animal trainers, as well as dancers. Both groups are thought to have migrated out of India around AD 1000.

Today the Romani people live widely throughout Europe, England, and the United States. Over the years since the Holocaust, many Romani have contributed greatly to the world of art, becoming famous musicians, artists, and writers. In particular, Ceija Stojka, who survived the Holocaust, was the first Romani to write a book about it: *We Live in Seclusion: The Memories of a Romni.*